CW00869411

MICHAEL HARDCASTLE

Roar to Victory

Illustrated by Patrice Aitken

MICHAEL HARDCASTLE

Roar to Victory

Containing *Roar to Victory, Fast From the Gate* and *Tiger of the Track*

DEAN

Dedicated, with love, to Barbara, who happily shared the adventures of scrambling.

Roar to Victory first published 1982
Fast From the Gate first published 1983
Tiger of the Track first published 1985
This edition first published 1992 by Dean
A division of Reed International Books Ltd
Michelin House, 81 Fulham Road, London SW3 6RB
Text copyright © Michael Hardcastle 1982, 1983 and 1985
Illustrations copyright © Patrice Aitken
1982, 1983 and 1985

A CIP catalogue record for this book is
available from the British Library

ISBN 0 603 55079 7

Printed in Great Britain by The Bath Press

Contents

Roar to Victory   7

Fast From the Gate   115

Tiger of the Track   225

MICHAEL HARDCASTLE

Roar to Victory

One

On the starting line Lee Parnaby tensed. He tried to crane forward over the handle-bars in the hope of spotting some significant movement on the part of the starter. A good start, a *flying* start, might make all the difference to his chances of success this time. But he had been drawn on the outside of the line of riders and he wasn't able to catch even a glimpse of the man who, at any second, would release the elastic tape.

Just above the heads of the twenty-two moto-cross riders a string of brightly coloured pennants fluttered fiercely in the disturbed air currents. Between the pennants hung numbered discs, each bearing the draw position of the rider stationed beneath it. Japanese and Italian engines quivered and behind the bikes clouds of blue exhaust fumes mushroomed and thickened. At their chosen and strategic points around the circuit spectators nervously bit their lips or offered up prayers or crossed fingers. Among them were parents or close relatives of most of the riders.

Lee hoped, most of all, that there wouldn't be a false start. Once, he himself had caused one, snapping the barrier as his bike seemed to take control of him. Then, when the riders had been recalled by the red flag and the race started properly, Lee's bike had unaccountably stalled and left him stranded. He remembered that as the most humiliating moment of his life.

Now, the tape catapulted sideways and the line instantly broke up as the riders surged forward. No recall flag was waving. The race had begun.

There had been a lot of rain early that morning and there were a few very soft patches of ground on the track. Lee had found one of them in an earlier race and slithered through it uneasily. Now, as the riders built up speed and approached the first bend, a sharp left-hander, the boy on Lee's left touched the edge of another boggy area. He reacted to the danger almost instantaneously; but, as he edged to his right, his front wheel flicked against Lee's knee.

Although the impact was only light Lee's bike wobbled momentarily; and then, neatly changing gear, he had it under control. His confidence suddenly soared as he accelerated towards the corner. Two other bikes had already collided fairly spectacularly on the far side of the track as the second wave of riders began to bunch.

10

The leaders, however, were clear by several metres and beginning to brake for the vital first bend. Whoever led the field at that point would have a considerable advantage. Glancing up, Lee spotted the yellow-and-black stripes of his brother's helmet. They were always easy to pick out at any stage of a race and Darren enjoyed being referred to as 'the Tiger of the Track'. Nonetheless, Darren's success still didn't match that of Graham Relton, the leader in their age-group. Graham had won both the earlier races that afternoon and clearly had made another fine start with the aim of completing a hat-trick. He and Darren went into that first left-hander with not a tyre's width between them.

Lee judged the moment well to change gear again and bump across the deepest of the ruts to avoid being crowded out by a pair of riders on his inside; he recognised one of them and knew that he was always a dangerous opponent in a tight squeeze for room. Yet Lee had managed to pull away from him comfortably.

With the field now well clear of that first bend and the leaders streaking towards the section that wended its way through the fringe of a wood, parents and the keenest supporters were dashing across the track. Most of them had been posted at, or just ahead of, the starting line in order to render immediate assistance if required. However, as

11

soon as their own riders were racing they headed for vantage points from which they could offer maximum vocal encouragement.

'Go on, Jason, get moving, get cracking!' a man in a red jacket was yelling as Lee passed by. 'Move, Jason, move! Don't drop back, whatever you do.'

Lee knew Jason quite well. They attended the same school. He knew that Jason would almost certainly never win a motocross in his life. He didn't even like riding a motor-bike. But his father had enough ambition for both of them and plenty to spare. Lee didn't have to look round to be aware that Jason would be gradually losing touch with the rest of the competitors.

Up ahead, Darren and Graham were still locked in deadly combat. As usual, Graham was riding with flair, saving valuable centimetres by knowing precisely which route to take through a corner or across a slope and still maintain top speed. His balance was exceptional, his style smooth and un-hurried. He never seemed to encounter unexpected problems. Graham was used to winning but his determination to win again was the equal of any-one's.

Darren, though, was staying with him at present. He was ready to take risks so as not to lose ground. But his hand on the throttle was sometimes un-steady and there was a constant jerkiness about his riding. Too much of the time he was thinking and worrying about what Graham might do next. He was fearful that Graham would suddenly dash so far ahead he couldn't be caught.

Greatly encouraged by his own good start, Lee settled down to some determined driving. This time he was going to move up on the leaders and remain with them. His greatest wish at the moment was to overtake Darren, to overtake him with a flourish so that Darren would know *at once* who'd passed him; he wanted everyone on the circuit to see that he, the younger brother, had gone ahead. Lee had vowed to himself that one day it would happen, and it might as well be today.

On the narrowest part of the track through the wood he had his first scare of the race. The rider in front of him just clipped one of the bales of straw piled against a tree trunk; the straw was intended to protect competitors but this particular bale was rather too solidly constructed. The Yamaha-mounted rider bounced back from the hay and, in his surprise, lost control of his machine. Suddenly it was sliding sideways across the track and directly in Lee's path.

Automatically, Lee braked – and turned his front wheel to go past the helpless rider on the left. There wasn't much of a gap to go through because by now the stricken motor-bike was practically broadside on to the oncoming riders. Yet, really quite neatly,

Lee managed to squeeze through, touching the offending bale of straw as he did so.

Already a marshal, stationed at that point for just such an occurrence, was leaping on to the track to wrestle with the sprawling Yamaha and get the rider back into the race.

'Well done, son,' he shouted to Lee. 'You're through! Keep going.'

A St John Ambulance man gave him a wave, too, and Lee's spirits were lifting again. He'd been on the edge of trouble but, by his own efforts, he had managed to avoid it.

All the same, he had lost ground on the leaders, as he noted when emerging from the wooded stretch. The circuit came back on itself at that point after describing a couple of 180-degree turns and thus Lee and those in his group appeared to be riding alongside the front runners; in fact, of course, they were on parallel lines.

By now Graham had pulled about a length ahead of Darren and the pair of them were almost a hundred metres ahead of the next rider. Some of the spectators were concluding that it was a two-bike race; and it sounded as though the majority were cheering Graham on to his hat-trick. Such favouritism, however, would merely act as another spur to Darren. But his expression was completely hidden behind his coloured visor. On the straight stretches, however, he was standing higher than usual so that the front wheel was doing no more than skip over the bumps. He himself believed he'd never ridden better.

On the first of the acute hairpins Lee cleverly used his leg for maximum guidance and in doing so he slipped past another rival. So far as he could tell he was now in sixth place, the best position he'd achieved in any race. He was feeling really good. Even the terrifying bomb-hole should be no great obstacle when he was riding like this, he told himself. He thought that was true. Well, perhaps very nearly true.

His bike was running well, too. In the past, he'd had trouble with the timing and he was sure that had cost him dear in some races. That was impossible to prove but it was what he felt. Uncle Ken, who did most of the mechanical servicing of the bike, had been rather dismissive about the trouble. But then, as Lee pointed out, it wasn't his uncle who rode in motocross.

Lee was rapidly approaching the second hairpin. Instinctively, he was in the act of changing down when another rider challenged on his inside. Lee hesitated – and then, to fight off his challenger, he accelerated. Almost immediately, he realised he would have to brake hard in order to negotiate the corner. His foot was late in coming down as a steering aid; and then the back wheel began to slide.

For a split second, he feared that everything was

out of control. He was barely aware of being over-taken by the boy who'd been challenging him. The first Lee saw of him was his back view as the erst-while rival pulled away with noteworthy efficiency. Nervously, Lee regained authority over his own machine and tried to regain his composure.

Quickly, he built up speed again. Yet he was furious with himself for reacting so amateurishly to the sudden presence of the boy who'd been cutting past him. The advantage at such a fierce bend had been with Lee himself because by steering a better course he could have blocked the challenge easily. Instead, he'd momentarily panicked and allowed the other boy to sweep past. He was forced to admit to himself that Darren would never have acted in that way.

There'd been a lot of movement by spectators, crossing from one viewing point to another as the race developed, but the majority of onlookers were perched on the rim of the famous bomb-hole. It really had been made by a bomb – one dropped by a German aircraft in the Second World War. For almost twenty-five years it had lain undetected be-neath the floor of a derelict factory. Then, when it came to light, the Army were called in to explode it under controlled conditions in a wide-open space. The piece of land chosen for the operation was the one now used by the Skalbrooke Schoolboy Motorcycle Club.

Lee felt he was going extremely well along the stretch that launched the riders into the heart-stopping depths of the crater. Once again, he was apparently beginning to overhaul the front runners, all of whom had now emerged from the bomb-hole. There was scattered applause as some boy cleverly skirted trouble on one of the steep slopes; and still louder cheers when he zoomed past another rider in mid air as they took the jump out of the crater together.

The pressure to do well was now at its most intense. Those competitors who hadn't fared too well in the day's earlier races were now absolutely determined to finish with a high position in order to have a chance of picking up a trophy. The awards were made only to the riders who filled the first ten places on the overall performances for the day. Graham Relton and Darren Parnaby were virtually guaranteed to pick up prizes but the battle was still on among the rest of the field for the vital points which would qualify them for a place in the order of merit.

'Go on, go *on*!' an irate father was screeching at a boy on a Suzuki which was slowing down just in front of Lee. For a moment, Lee thought the man was yelling at him. But then, as he swept past the struggling rider, he saw out of the corner of his eye that the Suzuki seemed to be troubled by wheel wobble. Lee even had time to wonder how the man could expect his boy to keep going when he had that sort of dire problem.

The ride was becoming exhilarating to Lee as he continued to make progress through the field. He barely hesitated, mentally or physically, as he reached the edge of the dreaded bomb-hole. At that point he was on his own: every other rider was either beyond the crater or well behind him.

It seemed to Lee that he just flew down the one-in-four gradient. He experienced a glow of excitement and achievement that touched almost every part of his body. With rare nonchalance he swerved round a log that somehow had tumbled into the bottom of the crater; and this time the cheers of the spectators were for him alone. Quite effortlessly, as he thought of it later, he roared up the far slope and then took off from the rim. He landed perfectly with the back wheel thrusting him powerfully forward again.

He had overcome his greatest fear; and now it hardly seemed to have been a fear at all.

The first circuit he completed in what was for him a record time. Once again he had the leaders in sight as he snaked into the wooded section. His concentration now was on overhauling Darren – and even, perhaps, Graham.

Lee saw the yellow flag far too late. It didn't register with his brain quickly enough that there was danger on that fierce S-bend through the trees.

19

The marshal was holding the flag rather than waving it because he was watching the ambulanceman attend to the rider still sprawled across the track.

Lee powered round the first curve and then, as he straightened up, saw the twin obstacles of fallen rider and horizontal bike.

He knew instantly that he could avoid only one of them.

Two

In spite of making a strenuous effort to miss the two obstructions by steering a path between them Lee cannoned into the front wheel of the fallen bike. Although everything happened very fast it registered with him that it was a Suzuki and that the unavoidable front wheel was still spinning. His own machine stopped dead on impact – and Lee was catapulted over the handle-bars.

The force with which he came down to earth knocked the breath out of his body. Although his first instinct was to get to his feet he found that he couldn't manage that for the moment. He simply gasped for air. Only when he was breathing again did he think about the damage he might have done to himself and his beloved bike.

The ambulanceman temporarily abandoned the unseated rider who'd caused the trouble in the first place and darted across to examine Lee. He'd noted the angle at which Lee had come down and his first

21

fear was that a shoulder had been dislocated. That sort of injury happened all too often to riders who were flung headlong from bikes which stopped abruptly.

His experienced, exploring fingers discovered no obvious disaster. Perhaps, he thought, the lad would be lucky enough to get away with just a few bruises and a shaking-up.

'How do you feel, son?' he inquired gently as Lee's eyes opened for the second time – and this time remained open.

'Er, I'm all right, I think,' was the tentative answer. Lee didn't like to admit to anything he wasn't sure of; but, equally, he hated to appear soft. In any case, his prime concern was the machine he'd been riding.

'Can you get up, then? You'll feel a lot better when you're on your feet,' the ambulanceman continued in a comforting vein. 'You're also still a bit in the way and the last thing we want is for you to get hit again.'

With the man's help, and then an arm round his shoulders, Lee stood up and moved away from the scene of the disaster. The marshal who'd been holding aloft the yellow flag had reacted smartly and wheeled Lee's bike off the track, while one of his companions dealt with the fallen Suzuki and its rider. Meanwhile, the race, of course, was going on as if nothing had happened and the leading machines zipped between the trees. By now Graham had pulled well ahead and there didn't seem to be much that Darren could do to make up the lost ground.

Lee stared in dismay at his motor-cycle. The green-and-silver paintwork no longer gleamed. The machine was smeared with mud and the exhaust appeared to be choked solid with the stuff; so no wonder the engine had cut out.

'How do you feel now, son?' the ambulanceman persisted as he watched the boy's reactions.

'Oh, well, my – er – my shoulder aches a bit – nothing bad, though,' confessed Lee, guessing that it might be best to admit to some minor ailment.

'Ah, well, it would do, wouldn't it, seeing as how you came down on it,' the man said with evident satisfaction. 'So you'll have to take things easy, now, son, and forget this race. Anyway, the leaders are already on the last lap. Nobody's going to catch *them*.'

Lee, vainly trying to remove all the sticking mud, just nodded. He'd known the moment he came off that the race was over for him. His luck was flat out again. What made it so awful this time, though, was that until the crash he'd been riding so masterfully.

'Better get hold of a friend to help you get the old bike back to the paddock,' the first-aid man was suggesting. 'With that dicky shoulder of yours you don't want to go lifting anything heavy.'

'There isn't anyone,' said Lee, without really

thinking of what he was saying. He was worrying about possible damage to the engine and the electrical system. The handlebars had taken the brunt of the fall.

'Oh, sorry, son!' The man looked embarrassed and anxious at the same time. 'But you're not on your *own*, are you? I mean, you must have *somebody* with you – if only to transport the old bike to and from the track.'

'There's Uncle Ken. But he'll be waiting for Darren to finish his race. Darren's my brother.'

'Oh, that's good! I mean, I'm glad somebody's looking after you, er – what did you say your name was, son? Lee. Ah, yes. Well, Lee, perhaps we should go and find this Uncle Ken now. Explain that you're all right. He's *bound* to be worried because he hasn't seen you come round the circuit again.'

'I don't suppose he'll really have noticed,' said Lee quietly.

The ambulanceman affected not to hear that comment. He had a word with one of the marshals and explained that he was going to accompany Lee, and his bike, to the paddock now that the Intermediates' race was practically over; he didn't think Lee ought to ride again that afternoon after the shaking he'd received.

Lee was aware of several rather scornful looks from spectators, both adults and boys of his own age, as they made their way to the paddock area which was close to the big public car park. Even if he couldn't ride it, he'd have preferred to push the bike himself but the ambulanceman wouldn't hear of it; so Lee, who sensed that he'd not win an argument, trailed silently along behind him. His shoulder ached a bit but he wasn't going to rub it.

'That's Uncle Ken over there, with my brother,' said Lee quickly as he caught sight of them. 'So I'll take the bike now, thanks, I'll be O.K.'

'Oh,' said the ambulanceman, his eyes opening wider. Lee knew exactly what was coming next; he'd heard it all too often in his life. 'You're twins, then? That must be –'

'No, we're not,' Lee replied, without any expression in his voice. 'He's one year and one day older than I am. So we're not even *nearly* twins. Actually, we're quite different in lots of ways.'

'Oh, well, your brother must be a bit small for his age,' remarked the ambulanceman softly. He had taken a liking to Lee and he hoped he hadn't upset him by mistaking the brothers for twins. 'Right, then, son, I'll leave you in your uncle's good hands. But if your shoulder gives you any real trouble get off to your doctor as fast as you can. Don't want to be laid up for the next Club meeting, do you?'

As he turned away he gave Lee a pat on his undamaged shoulder; and, at that moment, Ken

25

Wragby, who'd been deep in conversation with Darren, glanced up and saw them.

'Hello, Lee, what happened to you, then?' he inquired brightly.

'A bike got in my way,' said Lee as nonchalantly as possible.

'Oh, yeah, I've heard that one before!' Uncle Ken responded with a loud laugh. 'Same thing happened to Darren - a bike ridden by a lad called Graham. A bit useful in the old saddle, is Graham. But Darren's going to get his revenge next time, aren't you, Champ?'

Darren looked only marginally embarrassed at that declaration but he made no reply. Mr Wragby was devotedly examining Darren's new Yamaha. It seemed to Lee that so far his uncle hadn't given even half a glance at Lee's machine. Still, that gave him an opportunity to scrape some of the mud off the swingarm and the exhaust system.

For a few minutes Darren and Uncle Ken discussed the gears of the Yamaha (as far as Lee could tell, Darren was alleging some malfunction as he tried to change 'real fast' into higher gear). Gingerly, Lee tested his left shoulder muscles and found that they protested as he did so. He thought, though, that he should keep exercising them to prevent them from stiffening up. Perhaps it would be a good idea to have a hot bath that night - a decision that would impress his mother, if nothing

else. He just hoped that Darren didn't have the same idea; Lee resented having to share a bath, on top of everything else, with his elder brother.

'Right then, I think I know how to sort that little problem out,' Uncle Ken announced confidently. 'So let's pack up and get off home. No point in staying on to watch the last two races.'

It was he who took charge of Darren's bike while Lee wheeled his own machine to the car park in their wake. Thankfully, his shoulder didn't hurt too much. Just as they came up to their van they passed Graham Relton who was strolling by in the opposite direction.

'Congrats on your win, Graham,' Lee said with a grin. On his part, it was an automatic reaction.

'Oh, er, thanks,' Graham muttered, with a sidelong look at Darren and Uncle Ken.

'Thanks *very much*, Lee,' Darren said fiercely as soon as Graham was out of earshot. 'It's nice to know that your own brother is *glad* you lost! True family spirit, that is.'

'Don't be daft,' Lee responded quietly. 'I was just being polite. Graham's a nice guy.'

'So *nice* he tried to knock me off at Victor's Corner, that's all!' Darren raged. 'Shoved me off with his foot as I tried to cut inside. But, naturally, there wasn't a marshal there to see it. Anyway, they're all on Graham's side. Sure is the blue-eyed boy round here.'

'I've never seen him rough-ride anybody,' Lee pointed out. 'Sounds like an excuse to me.'

'Cut out the squabbling, you two!' Uncle Ken ordered as he heaved Darren's bike into the back of the old delivery van. Then, as he took hold of Lee's machine he added, 'You've let this get a bit mucky, haven't you? Get as much of that mud off as you can before we get home, Lee.'

'Sorry,' Lee murmured. He didn't feel apologetic, though. His uncle still hadn't bothered to ask what had happened to him in the race.

While Darren sat up front beside the driver Lee squatted awkwardly in the back and tried to remove as much of the mud as possible. The battered old van had served them well but now it was almost too small for them; and, indeed, Uncle Ken had promised that when they moved up to the Seniors at fourteen, and acquired more powerful bikes, he'd get a bigger vehicle.

Long before they reached his uncle's house in a village on the far side of Skalbrooke Lee was feeling thoroughly fed-up and tired. His arms had been aching even before he started on the cleaning operation. He made a firm promise to himself that he would step up his campaign to improve his stamina and overall fitness. To succeed in the tough and very competitive game of motocross a rider had to maintain peak fitness. Uncle Ken was always stressing that. Darren tended to scoff at that because he thought brains and riding skills were all that really counted; naturally, he believed he possessed both to a high degree. So he didn't bother with any of the muscle-building exercises and weight-training that Lee favoured. Quite regularly he told Lee he was crackers to go in for that stuff, and Lee said nothing in reply because he was accustomed to criticism from his elder brother.

Now, having removed the worst of the mud, he leaned back against the side of the van and listened to Uncle Ken and Darren plotting the downfall of Graham Relton at the next meeting of the Skalbrooke SMC. From the way Darren was talking it was plain that he didn't foresee any difficulty in getting in front, and *staying* in front, when he met his chief rival again. Lee rolled his eyes upwards when he heard that. It was a familiar story; Darren was always *promising* to do this or that – but somehow, when it came to the appointed day, he never quite succeeded in his intentions. But, *of course*, there was invariably a perfect excuse for his failure. Usually Darren had been the victim of another rider's cunning cheating . . . or he'd been terribly unlucky to suffer a mechanical failure . . . or a rival had collided with him accidentally and put him out of the race. Darren, according to Darren, never made simple mistakes himself. Things that went wrong were definitely somebody else's fault.

'You're very quiet, Lee,' said his uncle, swinging round to glance at him.

'Oh, er, yes,' Lee, startled, agreed. There hadn't been much opportunity to be anything else with Darren chatting away non-stop. 'I was, er, just thinking.'

'Thinking about food, I imagine. Well, I expect your aunt will have something good for us as usual. Won't be long now.'

Lee would have laughed if he'd felt in better spirits. For some reason he'd never been able to understand, his uncle had the idea that Lee was forever starving and therefore needed to be supplied with food in great quantities as often as possible. It was a complete fallacy. Lee's appetite was just normal and scarcely any bigger than Darren's. Yet their uncle wasn't constantly trying to force food down Darren's throat. Fortunately, Aunt Sue treated the matter as a bit of a joke and would say that Lee wasn't as skinny as that. Nonetheless, she always gave him a good portion of everthing and seemed pleased when he ate up.

While his uncle and Darren fussed about with the bikes in the workshop behind the house on arriving home, Lee went into the kitchen to get a drink of orange juice or anything else that would quench his sudden thirst. Sometimes they all had a meal almost immediately they returned from a meeting. On those occasions Uncle Ken took his nephews to their own home fairly early in the evening. He worked as a regional sales manager for a company that made canned foods, and occasionally he had to set off on a Sunday evening to be in time for a sales conference the following day.

'Ah, hello, Lee,' Aunt Sue greeted him cheerfully as she breezed into the kitchen. 'Had a good day? Pick up a trophy?'

'Er, no, not exactly. Actually, I came off and didn't even finish the race. My shoulder aches a bit but there's nothing wrong with it, really.'

Mrs Wragby gave him a calculating look. 'Um, well, you do look *a bit* grim – and a bit muddy, too.

31

Listen, why don't you treat yourself to a nice hot bath and soak any old aches and pains away? There's plenty of hot water and the meal won't be ready for at least an hour.'

'Oh, great! Yes, I'd really like that.'

She was both surprised and amused by his rapid acceptance of the offer. As he turned towards the stairs, she added, 'Oh, Lee, have you had any news this week from your Dad?'

'No.' That was his instant reaction. Then, relenting slightly, he said, 'Well, Mum had a postcard from Panama. Nothing for Darren or me – as usual.'

'Oh, well,' said Aunt Sue brightly. 'Perhaps his next leave will be a really long one and then he can spend lots of time with you. Now, then, I suppose I'd better go and have a word with those other motor-cycle maniacs and see what they're up to. Enjoy your bath, Lee.'

As he reclined in the luxuriously warm water and enjoyed the solitude, Lee found his thoughts drifting to his father, who was in the Merchant Navy, and wondering where his ship might be now. His communication with his family when he was away for months on end was infrequent, to say the least, but sometimes spectacular: he would telephone from the middle of an ocean in the middle of an English night. When that happened their mother would arouse Lee and his brother to have a few words with him, words all too often splintered by atmospherics or lack of concentration because the boys were still half asleep.

Yet, when he was at home, Brian Parnaby took remarkably little interest in the activities of his sons. It was his brother-in-law, Ken Wragby, who inspired and involved himself in their enthusiasms.

'Lee! Lee, are you awake in there?' a voice was calling; and a hand was slapping against the bathroom door. It was a moment before Lee realised who it was: Joanne, his cousin, almost a year younger than himself. 'Listen, Mum's sent you a mug of coffee. I've brought it for you. Shall I bring it in?'

'Er, no, no, thanks, Jo!' He sat up and shot an anxious glance at the door; and saw, to his relief, that he had remembered to lock it. 'The door's locked. Leave it outside, would you?'

She laughed. 'Oh, I was going to! 'Bye, then.'

He waited a minute or so and then went to retrieve the coffee. Then, just as he was taking the first sip, someone else banged heartily on the door.

'Hey, come on out of there,' yelled Darren. 'I want to use the bathroom.'

Lee looked at the locked door with immense satisfaction.

'Well, hard lines, Daz,' he called. 'This time, you'll just have to wait for me, won't you?'

Three

It had not been a good day, in any way, for Lee.
As, painstakingly, he completed a larger-than-life-
size drawing of the human eye, his mind wandered
over the events of the past few hours. His first
mistake of the day had been to smash a teapot,
his second to turn his back on a cricket ball that
must have been travelling at about a hundred
miles an hour. In addition to those mishaps, he'd
somehow managed to upset quite a number of
people.

For some reason, he'd overslept that morning,
perhaps because he'd had a restless night with dis-
turbing dreams. His mother, supposing wrongly
that Darren had awakened him because they slept
in the same room and Darren was already down-
stairs, hadn't come upstairs to tell him what time
it was and to hurry up. She, it turned out, had also
had a poor night and so wasn't in the best of moods.
Then, when he did belatedly come down for his

breakfast, he'd been in such a rush he'd knocked the china teapot flying with the swirling tail of his jacket. Uncompromisingly, his mother had insisted that he clean up the mess before going off to school, though Lee pointed out that he was going to miss his bus.

'You've missed your usual bus, so another one missed isn't going to make any difference,' she replied.

'Oh, Mum, that's not fair!' he protested.

'*Life's* not fair,' was her final comment.

That was already Lee's verdict and it was confirmed as soon as he arrived at school and collected two penalty points for being half-an-hour late – and then ran foul of the sports master who was taking Lee's class for cricket coaching.

Cricket wasn't a game that he cared for and Mr Burns guessed as much. So, when Lee dropped a relatively easy catch, he was ordered to field closer to the bat at the suicidal position of forward short leg. 'If you're nearer to the ball when it leaves the bat you might stand a chance of holding on to it,' snorted Mr Burns, who insisted on everyone taking every game and training session seriously. Unfortunately, the bowler dropped the ball short, the batsman swung powerfully, connected crisply – and Lee tried to get out of the way of the bullet-like shot. Luckily for him it was the fleshy part of the leg that took the impact but it was an exceedingly

35

painful blow. Lee had hopped about frantically but
Mr Burns was unsympathetic.

'I don't expect you put on a performance like
that when you fall off your motor-bike, Lee, so
there's no need for that sort of carry-on,' he said
sharply.

Several of the class had a good laugh at that; but
they were the ones, of course, who were deeply
envious of Lee's opportunities to compete in motocross events.

Even now, as the school day was dragging to a
close, Lee could still feel the effects of that crack on
the back of his thigh. There could be no doubt that

he would have a multi-coloured bruise by now. Of
course, it was hardly in a place where he could
examine its development at present. Still, he managed a grin at the thought of how he'd got out of
the firing line as a result of his injury: the sports
master had sent him to assist the groundsman to
roll the pitch. As luck had it, the groundsman was
a superbike fanatic and so they'd had a good chat
about the merits of various motor-cycles.

'Ah, you find the aqueous humour a subject for
some amusement of your own, do you, young Parnaby?' Mr Curzon, the biology teacher, asked with
sudden, and heavy, sarcasm. It was the sort of

witticism that some members of the class would appreciate, he knew, and he smirked at the dutiful laughs.

'Er, no, sir,' Lee replied carefully. He'd just labelled that part of the eye between the cornea and the lens and so he knew that aqueous humour was a fluid, nearly pure water, contained in that space. It was typical of Swearer, as everyone called Mr Curzon beyond his hearing, to pick on that word for his joke. 'I think my face must have, er, slipped.'

'Quite!' the biology teacher shot back instantaneously. 'You and I have never seen eye to eye, Lee!'

Once again his remark triggered off a volley of more laughs and even cheers. It seemed to Lee that Swearer was trying to win back his popularity with the class. Earlier in the double period he had exploded with rage because some boys had fooled about during an experiment involving the cutting up of a dead animal. The whole class had been punished with a written test so hard that nobody could manage to get more than half the answers right. So the outcome of that was to be another test, later in the week, for which they would have to do extra homework. What was so infuriating to Lee was that he hadn't been even remotely involved in the dissection of the vole; but everyone had to suffer because of the stupidity of one small group.

As soon as Swearer Curzon had turned away to

torment somebody else about the location of the 'blind spot' in the eye – where the optic nerve leaves the retina – Lee took a surreptitious glance at his watch. Only another five minutes to go and then the school day would be over. He had it in mind to go along to the leisure centre and make use of the multi-gym: he was anxious to strengthen the muscles in his arms and legs to help his riding and improve his stamina. Since the last meeting of the Skalbrooke SMC when he'd crashed into the Suzuki almost a fortnight had gone by; but, because of homework and essential jobs he'd had to do around the house there had been few opportunities to do much training.

Piercingly, the final bell rang.

Half the class clattered to their feet immediately, calling to one another or scrambling to be the first to reach the door. None of them managed it. Swearer planted himself in front of the exit and ordered everyone to sit down again. He looked, as someone remarked later, livid. For almost a minute he told them what he thought of them; and for several minutes they sat in complete silence. Even when Swearer did at last let them go they had to file out without a word being spoken.

Lee dashed for the front entrance of the building the split-second he was clear of the classroom. He'd promised to meet Bobbie Keenan and repay him the pound he'd borrowed the previous day. Bobbie was the sort of lad who always had money to spare and so when Lee somehow lost his dinner money Bobbie was the obvious one to approach for a loan. Unfortunately, with over-sleeping and being in such a rush that morning Lee had forgotten to ask his mother for some extra money; and thus, at dinnertime, he'd had to borrow from Darren to repay Bobbie's loan.

'Oh, it's O.K., it didn't really matter today,' Bobbie remarked casually when Lee paid the money over and apologised for being late.

'Oh no,' said Lee earnestly, 'I hate being in debt.'

As, thankfully, he started on his way home at last, Lee thought about the money situation. While it was true that he disliked owing anything he knew that he was sometimes very careless about money. He never worried about it and didn't often even think about it. If he had money, that was fine; if he had none, well, that was just too bad. Darren, on the other hand, always had money, however much he spent, and he knew to the penny how much was in his pocket at any given moment. Even when today's loan to his brother was repaid, Darren would remember for a very long time exactly how much, and for how long, Lee had borrowed from him.

Because he was absorbed by his thoughts Lee didn't immediately notice the scuffle taking place just ahead of him in Boston Grove. It was a narrow, tree-lined thoroughfare that provided a short cut on the way to the bus stop. Its only notable feature was a half-derelict Methodist church, surrounded by tall railings and flanked by an alleyway that led to a row of terraced houses. For anyone wanting to set an ambush it was an ideal spot.

Suddenly Lee became aware that a couple of boys were rushing across the road from the entrance to the church. He recognised one of them as Andy Haylin, a loud-mouthed, beefy character who was going to win every event he entered on sports day – according to him. His father had been a third-class professional wrestler in his time and Haylin was always relating the story of how he'd once won a contest on television.

'Right, then, Parnaby, let's see you scramble up there,' he was yelling. 'That will show how good *you* are!'

Then he grabbed his mate round the shoulders and together they leaned back against the wall facing the church and guffawed.

Lee drew level with the entrance and, glancing down the flagged path, saw his brother standing by the porch. With a forlorn expression, Darren was staring up at the sharply sloping roof. Lying against the tiles at such an angle it might almost have been stuck there by super-glue, was a briefcase. Even without Darren's presence, Lee would have had no difficulty in identifying its owner. The case, in soft

41

calfskin with brass locks, was probably his brother's second most prized possession. Like the first, his motor-cycle, it had been a gift from Uncle Ken.

'Why is it up there?' Lee asked quietly, coming up behind Darren.

His brother swung round, his eyes now flashing angrily as he caught sight of Haylin and his accomplice.

'Because that stupid pair of maniacs are jealous, that's why! They can't win anything off their own bat so they try to bring everyone down to their own rotten level. They heard me talking about scrambling so they chucked the case up there.' He stopped and then added in a whisper, 'Lee, how did they know I can't stand heights?'

'I don't suppose they did. I expect it's just Haylin's way of trying to make things as difficult as possible. Typical of him. Anyway, I'll get it for you – if I can reach it. You know climbing doesn't bother me.'

Lee was sizing up the task as he spoke. The idea of scaling rock faces had always appealed to him when he saw climbers in action on television; but he'd not had an opportunity of finding out whether he was really capable of it. The best he'd achieved was in an old quarry when he'd climbed several metres to retrieve a child's escaped kite: that had been much easier than he'd imagined.

42

'It's a bit sheer, isn't it?' Darren pointed out uneasily. 'I mean, what can you get a grip on?'

'Well, there's that bit of drainpipe up there, if it hasn't rusted too badly. The bricks aren't in good shape, so they'll be easier to grasp. You watch to see if anything shows signs of breaking up. O.K.?'

'Look, Lee, I think I'd better see if I can borrow a ladder or something. I mean, if anything happens, Mum'll go mad – mad with me. And –'

'Just watch, Daz, just watch. We're not giving Haylin a free load of laughs.'

The easiest part of the whole operation was to get up on to the wide sill of the ground-floor window and Lee didn't even need to ask for any assistance. The glass had disappeared long ago in an outbreak of vandalism and the opening had been boarded up with the sort of efficiency that ensured no one would get in without a lot of hard effort. Lee grasped one of the struts, pulled himself up and then stepped sideways along the sill towards the drainpipe.

'It looks a bit risky to me, Lee,' his brother said worriedly.

Lee just shrugged, which in itself was a slightly hazardous gesture to make. He guessed he looked more confident than he felt but now he'd launched himself into the recovery business he wasn't going to give up without very good cause.

The pipe seemed to be secure. With one hand on

43

the pipe and the other on the projecting bricks that formed the decorative arch of the window, he quickly gained height. He was very thankful that the shoes he was wearing had rubber soles – and ribbed rubber at that.

From the other side of Boston Grove there came a faint cheer that was intended to be ironic. But it sounded half-hearted. Andy Haylin and his confederate were rapidly concluding that their victim's brother was a pretty determined character. They knew a great deal about their class-mates but hardly anything about the younger boys at the school. So they had no idea what Darren's brother was really like; and they'd made the mistake of assuming he was exactly like Darren.

Lee barely heard them. He was concentrating completely on transferring his weight from the top of the window arch to a secondary drainpipe which forked away from the main pipe at the convenient angle of about 45 degrees. If he could gain a foothold on that he should then be able to make excellent progress towards the roof.

He was just about to swing himself across to the pipe when Haylin yelled as loud as he could manage, 'You'll never make it, kiddo! That pipe won't hold even your skinny weight. You've had it!'

His sole intention was to unnerve Lee and he very nearly succeeded. The climber made the elementary error of trying to glance towards the

44

speaker. His searching right foot missed its toe-hold and next moment was scrabbling desperately across the face of the wall.

Darren's face lost its colour in an instant. He clenched his fingers so tightly the nails bit into the palms.

'Pack it in now, Lee,' he called in anguish. 'I don't care about the case. Just leave it and get down! I mean it.'

Lee's right shoe at last wedged itself against a bracket. He paused and expelled a long breath. The worst was over. He was sure of that. For a moment, he'd thought he was going to fall. Now he felt quite safe again. Lee wouldn't allow himself to be distracted again by anything – or anyone. His determination to reach the briefcase had simply been increased by Haylin's stupid call. He had barely heard Darren's voice.

The rest of the route to the roof presented no problems at all. After testing the guttering and finding it ready to drop off at any moment he edged his way to the far wall and pulled himself on to the tiles from that direction. The angle of the roof was steep enough for him to decide to lie flat against the tiles – and then wriggle his body across to the briefcase. He was calm and confident; he could even think about those watching him and guess that *they* were supposing he was terrified.

Within a minute he had reached his objective.

45

With his outstretched left hand he grasped the corner of the case and pulled it towards him. Then, taking hold of the handle, he yelled, 'Here it comes, Daz! Don't drop it now.'

With a flick of his wrist he sent the briefcase spinning up over the guttering in a neat arc. Darren moved a couple of paces and then took the case into his arms like a rugby full-back receiving the ball from a high kick.

'Got it!' he called to his brother. 'Well done, Lee.'

Then he turned round to see the reaction of Haylin and his pal. But the ex-wrestler's son and his fellow thug had vanished. Darren could smile again. With Lee's help, he'd defeated them.

'Thanks, kiddo,' he said warmly when Lee reached the ground. He even went so far as to put his arm round his brother's shoulders. 'I'll do something for you when I get the chance.'

'O.K.,' Lee said, shrugging. 'I'll hold you to that one day.'

As they strolled out of Boston Grove, however, Lee was thinking that he didn't care whether Daz repaid the debt. In a way, he hoped it would be forgotten – well, no, not forgotten, exactly, but perhaps ignored until it was necessary to use it as an advantage in some way. The one thing he himself would have to remember was to repay Darren the money he'd borrowed in order to pay Bobbie.

46

Darren, now swinging his briefcase contentedly, didn't keep him company for long. Spotting some of his cronies as they rejoined the main road he simply said, 'See you when we get home, Lee,' and then dashed away. In recent years it had become plain to Lee that Darren couldn't bear to be seen with a younger boy, even if that boy was his brother. Odd, really, but that's how it was, as Lee had pointed out to his own friends who expressed surprise about the relationship.

When, at last, he dropped off the bus close to his home, his thoughts were fixed on his training session that evening at the local leisure centre. Perhaps it was time to alter his routine in the weight-lifting exercises so that he could try to build up –

'Hey, don't I get so much as a grin from you today, young Lee?' a familiar voice interrupted his planning.

'Oh, er, hello, Mr Thirlwell. Sorry I didn't notice you.'

'Nor would you have done if I hadn't spoken up. Deep down you were in some rare old thoughts. Homework is it, that's bothering you?'

Mr Thirlwell was a travelling greengrocer with a van that was said to be older than he was. Darren had once described it, rather contemptuously, as a shoebox on four wheels. Rectangular it certainly was, with just the cab and the snub-nose engine to break up the severe lines, but Mr Thirlwell kept it

in beautiful condition. There never seemed to be a speck of dirt to mar its orange and chocolate-brown paintwork and the brass handles on the doors gleamed with polish. Its owner and Lee had been friends for years, ever since the day, in fact, when Lee, standing beside his mother as she bought vegetables and fruit, announced loudly to the world that the van was 'the smartest and bestest car in the whole world.' His immediate reward had been a ride in the 'bestest' along the entire length of the street, during which journey he had taken alternate bites of the apple and the banana that had also been given to him by the delighted owner-driver.

'No, no, homework's no worry,' replied Lee, leaning against the side of his favourite vehicle. 'Haven't got any for tonight. It's my get-fit training I was thinking about – you know, to make me a *stronger* rider. To improve my stamina, really.'

'What you need is vitamins, young Lee. Vitamins – and plenty of 'em. They'll give you all the stamina you need.' Mr Thirlwell was warming to a favourite theme and Lee hastily stopped leaning and prepared to bolt. 'Now, take my lemons and oranges, for instance. Just packed full of Vitamin C, they are, and –'

'Sorry, Mr Thirlwell, I've just got to dash! I'm already late for tea and Mum gets really mad, you see. Oh yes, and my cousin'll be here, so I've got to entertain her, that's what Mum says. . .'

The greengrocer shook his head sadly as Lee, still trying to offer excuses over his shoulder, sped along the avenue. He'd been going to present the lad with a few of his vitamin-packed oranges to boost his suspect stamina.

Four

'I am beginning,' said Mrs Parnaby stonily, 'to despair of you, Lee. You'd turned it into a ruinous day before you left for school this morning – and now it looks as though you're trying to end it on the same note. Well, it's not good enough.'

For a few moments she buttered slices of bread in tight-lipped fury. Lee could only wait apprehensively for the next onslaught. He rather feared that she might decide he wasn't to be allowed any tea at all. If that happened, he didn't think he would survive the rest of the day.

'You could surely see this instructor at the gymnasium on some other evening, couldn't you?' his mother continued relentlessly. 'There *are* other evenings in the week when he could give you the undoubted benefit of his expertise, I'm certain. So –'

'No, he *isn't* there every night, Mum,' Lee cut in. 'It's tonight when he's able to *help* me with the weights in the right ratios. It's all *fixed*, he *told* me what time to be there.'

His first statement was true; the second would not have stood up to a severe examination by anyone who knew all the facts. Lee could only pray that his mother wouldn't spot any flaws.

'Well, if that's the arrangement then you'd better go,' she announced heavily. 'I don't want you to earn a reputation for letting people down. Though you've certainly let Joanne down. So you'd better go straight through and apologise to her. And tell her that tea's almost ready. Go on.'

He went through into the lounge where Joanne was watching television. She visited them once a week, though not always on the same day, for a meal. That was one way, Mrs Parnaby had explained, of repaying the hospitality and generosity of the Wragbys to Darren and Lee.

'Jo, I'm sorry about this, but I've just got to go out tonight,' he told her with what he thought was a convincing display of disappointment. In fact, he really did like his cousin and usually they got on well together. 'So I'm afraid you'll have to, er, amuse yourself.'

'Well, that won't be difficult. I'm used to it,' she replied brightly. 'You always are when you're an only one.'

Lee ran his hand through his helmet of hair that was the colour of honey. 'Yeah, I know how you feel. It's like that here most of the time. I mean, I didn't even *know* Daz was going out to tea tonight at one of his mates. But I get the blame for not looking after you.'

'I expect younger ones are always the ones that suffer,' remarked Joanne with an understanding smile. 'At least I'm spared that! I expect it's something special you are going out to, isn't it, Lee?'

He told her about his plans to build up his stamina so that when he rode in motocross he wouldn't get tired however tough the course and however severe the conditions. As ever, Joanne listened attentively and asked only intelligent questions. Lee knew that she didn't discuss such matters with Darren; his brother had no time for her. Lee thought she knew a great deal about bikes and scrambling. No doubt she picked most of it up from listening to her father, though Uncle Ken normally didn't say much to her when Lee and Darren were there.

'Well, anyway, there's something good on television tonight, so I'll enjoy that instead,' Joanne said reassuringly when Lee's mother raised the matter of his departure for the umpteenth time during the meal.

'That's great, Jo,' he responded gratefully. 'And I'll make it up to you soon – take you somewhere special you'd like to go.'

'You will that,' his mother added firmly.

As he hurried down the avenue after leaving the house Lee couldn't help feeling guilty about the way he'd abandoned Joanne; and he was thankful that she hadn't asked to come and watch him doing his training. It was a wonder his mother hadn't suggested that, but perhaps she considered that a gymnasium was no place for a young girl. Lee suspected, though, that Jo would have enjoyed the experience.

He was waiting impatiently for the bus to arrive when, without warning, a passing vehicle suddenly swerved towards the kerb and then screeched to a

halt a couple of metres from where Lee was standing. The next instant a familiar face was grinning at him through the passenger's window and calling to him to get a move on. Greg Shearsmith, a fellow motocross rider, was forever in a hurry.

'Where you going, then?' Greg demanded to know. Then, when he'd been given an answer, he immediately countered, 'Oh, that's no good, Lee! The only training that's any good is on the bike. Got to ride all the time to be a winner. Right, Dad?'

'Right, son,' confirmed Mr Shearsmith, sitting behind the steering wheel of the Volkswagen minibus. 'So let's get going, O.K.? Give your pal here a lift and talk on the way.'

'Thanks very much,' said Lee, climbing in. It occurred to him that he'd be saving a bus fare besides getting to his destination faster.

'Look, don't bother with that weight-lifting rubbish tonight,' Greg resumed as soon as they were moving. 'I could use a bit of help, so come and do some bike training with me. We're testing my new bike – it's on the trailer. But it's under wraps because we don't want too many people to see what we've done.'

Lee hesitated. The idea was tempting; but, on the other hand, he didn't much care for Greg, an aggressive, almost bullying, type who thought nothing of literally knocking other riders out of his path in scrambles. Occasionally, though, he rode quite brilliantly. His father was known to be well off and, just as usefully, a skilled mechanic.

Greg, who had the shortest haircut of any boy Lee had ever seen, was looking at him with an eagerness for a favourable answer that Lee found surprising.

'Lee, I know you haven't got your own bike now because you keep it at your uncle's, right?' he rushed on. Lee just nodded. 'So, O.K., maybe you can have a go on mine – we'll see how it works out. But Dad's got this meeting he can't get out of so he can't do the timing and that sort of stuff. He'll come and pick us up later and get you home again. You can do your own riding a lot of good by coming with me and training where it matters – on the track, on a *bike*. A real racer, too.'

Lee hastily buried his doubts.

'O.K., then, Greg. It's true, I do miss not having my machine at home. The garden's not big but I could get *a bit* of riding practice. Did you say you had a *new* bike? What is it?'

'A Shearsmith Special!' Greg declared to Lee's astonishment. 'Yeah, honest! Dad's designed it himself and it's great – I absolutely know it's going to be the greatest bike Skalbrooke's ever seen. But it's all secret until I ride it at the next meeting in a fortnight.'

'Well, I'll know a lot about it if you let me try it

out tonight,' Lee pointed out. 'So it won't exactly be a secret then, will it?'

'Oh, but I can trust *you*, Lee,' was Greg's reply to that.

Rather to his own surprise, Lee was pleased by that compliment. He began to see Greg Shearsmith in a different light. Perhaps the rest of the club members had been misjudging him and mistaking his enthusiasm for win-at-all-costs aggression. It was certainly both sporting and generous of him to allow another rider – a rival – to train on his new, and obviously very special, machine.

They fell to discussing the previous meeting of the Skalbrooke SMC and it wasn't until Mr Shearsmith brought the Volkswagen to a halt and switched off the engine that Lee realised where they'd been heading.

'We're at the Autodrome!' he exclaimed. 'But we can't practise here, Greg – it's where the next meeting is being held. It's against the rules to ride on a circuit before a meeting.'

'Ah, but we're being cunning, aren't we?' Greg replied with a note of satisfaction in his voice. 'We're not going to go on the track itself, just *along-side* it. Nothing in the rules to say we can't do that. Right, Dad?'

'Right, son,' said Mr Shearsmith, disappearing behind the minibus to unhitch the trailer. Greg followed eagerly, Lee glumly. He felt he ought to ask Mr Shearsmith to take him back into town but, somehow, he thought the man would refuse. If Greg wanted Lee's assistance, Greg would have it. His father would see to that.

With loving care, the new bike was removed from its stand on the trailer; and Lee couldn't help feeling envious when he studied it.

'You like it, then?' inquired Greg, letting his fingers trail tenderly over the gleaming black paint of the fuel tank, and then caress the fabric, equally black, of the saddle. Lee just nodded. Mere words seemed inadequate.

'It's the exhaust system that makes it so special,' Greg continued, stooping to pat the ringed barrel attached to the exhaust pipe. 'I get a wider spread of power, you see. And a bit extra on top speed. Dad's brilliant at tuning and getting a different power delivery.'

'So you'd better match that brilliance with your riding,' said Mr Shearsmith crisply as he nipped back into the minibus. 'Don't do anything daft, Greg. Don't draw attention to yourself. You never know who may be wandering over the Autodrome – courting couples, bird watchers, poachers with shotguns. So be careful. I'll be back as soon as I can. Cheers, then!'

Greg was plainly pleased to see him go, so that he could get on with the business of riding. He waited, though until the Volkswagen was out of

58

sight before putting on his kit. From helmet, to new leathers with knee protector caps, to smooth-soled boots, he dressed slowly, enjoying the feel and fit of every item. It was quite a theatrical performance and Lee watched in some amusement. Already it had occurred to him that if he was to be given a ride, he would have to borrow some of Greg's kit as, of course, he had none of his own with him.

'I thought your Dad would have wanted to stay to see how you got on,' he observed. 'I mean, he's pretty keen on your riding – and the bike.'

Greg adjusted the body-belt which he wore under his leathers to protect his kidneys in the event of a bad fall. 'I know,' he agreed, 'but this meeting of his is about finance and he's the treasurer, so he didn't have any option. Anyway, he's had a go himself on the Shearsmith Special so he *knows* it's terrific. And, naturally, he knows I'm a terrific rider! So he doesn't need to act like a – like a watchdog.'

The ebony special throbbed into exciting life and Greg bobbed away at a surprisingly sedate speed. Lee watched as his old rival – though now, he supposed, Greg would have to be accepted as a new friend – went round in a wide sweep as if to demonstrate what excellent balance he possessed. The turf was springy and quite dry, for the Autodrome was on the edge of wide moors across which winds were forever sweeping. At one time it had been an Air Force base and remnants of the runways and taxi-ing paths were still used occasionally for motor-racing events, particularly on bank holidays.

The Schoolboy Motor-cycle Club paid a fee to use the place and its facilities on a regular basis, and thus had been permitted to construct their own circuit within the boundaries formed by the runways. Because some excavations had been carried out in one area during a search for ancient remains, one or two hollows had formed and deepened during the years of neglect; and, inevitably, they had been incorporated into the club's circuit. There were no trees but a handful of impenetrable bushes constituted the major hazards so far as vegetation was concerned.

It was a very fast track. Oval in design, it contained two long, undulating straights along which riders of Greg's nature were bound to score on the basis of speed alone. But it also featured a couple of V-turns: and those V's, as someone had remarked, stood for Vicious. The bikes had to be more or less 'walked' round those bends.

'Right, what do you think of the Special, then?' Greg called out as he rode back towards Lee after completing another wide circle, this time in an anti-clockwise direction.

'Looks great,' Lee admitted.

'It *feels* great,' Greg enthused, boosting the

61

engine note to a healthy roar. 'Now I'll show you what we can do together.'

For a moment, Lee supposed Greg was referring to some sort of partnership between them; but then it became clear that he was talking about himself and his bike. From some concealed pocket he produced a stopwatch and handed it over.

'I'm going to do one circuit just to warm up,' he explained. 'Then, second time round I want you to time me. You can station yourself at V-One and put the clock on the moment I come out of that turn. Then later on, when I go again I'll be out to beat my first record. O.K.?'

'Well, all right,' Lee said a trifle doubtfully. 'But I thought you promised me a ride sometime.'

'Oh sure,' Greg replied nonchalantly as he pulled his goggles into place. 'But I've got to set that top time first. Better get yourself off to V-One, Lee, 'cos it won't take me long to get there, you know.'

With a splendid eruption of blue smoke, the Shearsmith Special surged away and in a matter of moments the rider was motoring at full chat. As he turned on to the circuit, Greg hadn't a care in the world.

Frowning, Lee made his way to the acute bend known to every club member as V-One. He couldn't suppress the feeling that Shearsmith was simply intending to employ him as a timekeeper.

As the scintillating Special disappeared from

62

sight and the engine note faded Lee thought he heard, distantly, the bark of a dog. He scanned the horizon but could see no sign of any animal. Dogs, he was well aware, could be a real problem to motor-cyclists if they took a dislike to bikes for any reason. So far the Autodrome had appeared to be deserted and he was keeping his fingers crossed that it would stay that way.

By now Lee was in the middle of the circuit and he turned to watch Greg flash by on the first of the straights. Greg was confident enough to give him a wave – and at that point he was actually crouching low in the saddle to cut down wind resistance. Lee guessed that the Special could be approaching a speed of 50 m.p.h.; but Greg wouldn't be able to sustain that much longer. Already he was leaning into a curve.

Lee descended into the slight dip where V-One was located. Not for the first time he thought what a fearful turn it was.

One half-minute of blissful peace he had all to himself. In the next half-minute or so, everything seemed to happen.

He looked to his left as he heard the noise of the Special's engine. It seemed to Lee that Greg really ought to be slowing down by now to negotiate the notorious bend in safety. Then, just as Greg began to brake, a small dog hurtled over the low banking and rushed straight at the bike.

63

Somehow, and it was to his great credit, Greg managed to swerve away from the dog, a short-haired terrier. In doing so, however, he lost control; and, as he fell off, the bike charged up the slope on its own before losing momentum. Greg, momentarily stunned, lay where he had fallen, with the dog snapping at his helmet.

Lee, seeing what would happen next if he didn't prevent it, darted across the track and up the incline. The bike was now slithering back towards Greg, and would have crashed into him and the dog if Lee hadn't grabbed the handle-bars and heaved

with all his strength. To his great relief, he arrested its ominous progress.

Suddenly, two men appeared above the banking – and, as they stared at the scene below, one of them began to call off the dog.

At that moment Greg sat up, pushed back his helmet and yelled, 'You stupid fools! Don't you realise it's murder to let a dog loose on a racing track?'

Lee glanced at the men to see their reaction and froze. He was so astounded he almost dropped the Shearsmith Special.

One of the men was Mr Cantrill, secretary of Skalbrooke SMC and a figure of total authority. He ran the club with enthusiasm and efficiency but no one ever defeated him in an argument. His word was law.

By now, Greg had realised who he was insulting. He swallowed hard and then fell silent. The dog, now that its anger was exhausted, disdainfully trotted away and went to sniff at Lee's ankles.

'I wouldn't have believed that you would flout our rules in such a deplorable fashion, Gregory,' Mr Cantrill told him coldly. 'You know very well that no member is allowed to practise on the track itself before the day of the meeting – yet here you are, riding at a foolhardy speed, risking not only your own life and limb but that of an innocent dog!'

'But that dog shouldn't –' Greg, having found his voice, tried to interrupt.

'Silence!' the secretary thundered. 'Don't add to your crimes by trying to make excuses. There *are* no excuses to be made in a situation of this nature. If you don't know what the punishment is for this crime, then you're about to learn what it is. You are banned from the club's next meeting. Not just from riding – from attending it as well. If you are so witless as to try to sneak in, as you sneaked in here this evening, then the ban will be extended for the rest of the season. Now, do you understand?'

Greg was too stunned to be able to reply. He

nodded because there was no alternative. His helmet on his head again, he turned away to examine the state of the Shearsmith Special following its slide down the incline.

Lee, believing that he had escaped the secretary's wrath, was about to offer Greg his sympathy when Mr Cantrill spoke again.

'The same penalty will apply to you, Lee Parnaby,' was the fierce judgement.

'But why, Mr Cantrill?' the victim asked. His sense of horror matched Greg's.

'For what the courts, I believe, would describe as aiding and abetting. You may not have been riding while I was watching but I don't doubt that was your intention. In any case, it was your duty to *prevent* Gregory here from breaking the rules, not to connive at wrong-doing.'

'But, Mr Cantrill – '

'There is *no* appeal against our sentence,' said the secretary, swiftly cutting off Lee's protest. 'If you aren't aware of the rules then go and read them. Now, be off, both of you – and try to show good sense in future.'

Until they were out of sight of the two men, the boys didn't speak. But Lee noticed that Greg's knuckles, as he gripped the handle-bars of the Special, were white.

'What rotten luck!' Greg exploded, when they were in sight of the boundary road where his father was to pick them up. 'To come here on the one night Cantrill was strolling about with a mate! That must have been his mate's dog, too, because Cantrill doesn't have a dog – doesn't even like 'em much because they have a habit of attacking motorcyclists. I heard him say so when he told a spectator off at a meeting. Tell you what, I wish my Dad had stayed with us – he wouldn't have let Cantrill ban us on the spot.'

Lee made no reply. He was thinking that if he'd stuck to his original plan for the evening, he wouldn't have been anywhere near the Autodrome. In a way, he was really being punished for not keeping his appointment in the gymnasium.

'Still, I found out one thing,' Greg continued. 'The special is a really fantastic bike. I reckon it'll beat anything on the track – anything.'

'Maybe,' said Lee. 'But that's no good if you're not allowed on the track in the first place, is it? I mean, in a club race.'

Greg glared at him – and then retaliated, 'Well, you won't be winning anything at the next meeting, either, will you? Still, that's normal for you.'

Five

Two weeks later, on the day of Skalbrooke SMC's next meeting, Lee Parnaby and his cousin Joanne were on their way to the Great Lingdale Show. Jo, whose idea it was, couldn't conceal her delight; and, gradually, as the bus drew nearer to the showground, Lee began to feel that he might manage to enjoy the outing, too.

Nonetheless, he couldn't help thinking about what might be happening that afternoon at the Autodrome. As usual, Darren had gone off to the meeting with the highest hopes of winning the Intermediates' races and so getting his revenge at last on Graham Relton. 'I'll give you a lap-by-lap description of how I became the champion,' Darren had promised. Lee had just raised his eyebrows, shrugged and made no audible comment. He was rather thankful that Darren had stopped breaking into peals of laughter whenever the subject of the ban on Lee's attendance at the meeting was mentioned.

Mrs Parnaby had tended to share Darren's attitude; she'd told Lee that he deserved his fate because he should have been at the gymnasium, especially after he'd abandoned his cousin for that reason. Uncle Ken was reasonably sympathetic but, unlike Mr Shearsmith, had not offered to contact the secretary in the hope of getting the ban lifted. Privately, Lee believed that if Darren had been the offender their uncle would have been frantic in his efforts to smooth things over with Mr Cantrill. Probably, however Uncle Ken had realised he had no hope of succeeding where Mr Shearsmith had failed, even though Lee's offence was hardly in the same category as Greg's.

'Missing one meeting will just make you all the keener to do well at the next one,' Uncle Ken had insisted with what Lee easily recognised as a fairly feeble attempt to boost his morale. 'When you hear how Darren's got on you'll be trying harder than ever to emulate him.'

Joanne had said nothing at the time but he had sensed her sympathy; and then, later, she had commented that he'd obviously been treated most unfairly. She had a low opinion of Greg, anyway, and thought it was typical of him not to try to take all the blame on himself and so persuade the officials to let Lee compete. Then, the following week during her visit to the Parnabys' for tea, she had come up with the idea of visiting the Great Lingdale

Show which would be taking place at the same time as the club's meeting. She'd pointed out that one of the highlights would be 'A breathtaking display of skill and daring by an internationally-famed team of motor-cycle riders from Germany' (well, that was how the official programme described the event); and, in addition, there would be 'A brilliant exhibition of high-speed cutting and balancing by Canadian axe-men'.

'Sounds all right, I suppose, but none of it will be as good as actually *riding* in the motocross,' was Lee's response as he handed back Joanne's advance programme.

'Oh, I know,' she agreed, 'but at least it'll take your mind off what you're missing, Lee. And I'll try not to be a bore while we're together.'

His mother, of course, thought it was a splendid suggestion; she, coming in at that moment, had caught sight of the programme. One glance at it was enough.

'This is your chance to make it up to Joanne,' she said crisply. 'It's where she wants to go. So you're both going – and I don't want to hear a word of complaint from you, Lee.'

So Lee had surrendered. There didn't seem much point in battling on against such odds. All the same, he knew that however good the show might be, he'd spend most of his time thinking about Darren's chances of a victory at last that

71

afternoon. If his brother *did* somehow manage to get a first he'd be absolutely impossible to live with for ever more; and at school everybody would know . . .

'Come on, Lee, snap out of those miserable thoughts!' Joanne said gaily as she steered him into the showground. 'I don't know *exactly* what you're thinking but I can make a jolly good guess. Look, the sun is shining, we've got money to spend, there's not a soul to tell us what we've *got* to do, so let's enjoy ourselves. Let's have a really *great* time. Tell you what, I'll buy you an ice-cream to start things off.'

So, contentedly licking chocolate-flake cornets, they went to stare at pens of sheep and pens of prime, snuffling porkers; at cages of drowsy rabbits and striding, strident cockerels; and to applaud the clever, precisely controlled driving by waggoners in charge of pairs of high-stepping shire horses in a competition held in the main show ring.

The next entertainment was to be one of the highlights of the day: the demonstration of their extraordinary and inventive talents by the axe-wielders from Canada. In common with the vast majority of spectators, Lee and Joanne had seen nothing like it anywhere. The men, dressed in trousers and singlets that displayed ample biceps, stood on huge logs and energetically cut them in half *between their feet* – and, what's more, did the cutting at the fastest speed possible because they were in competition with each other to be the first to finish and jump down from the bisected log. One false slash and it could have been a foot that was removed, not a chunk of wood. But every axeman emerged from that contest quite unscathed.

Then the men split up into pairs to form three teams – and this time it was very solid-looking blocks of wood – thicker than telegraph poles – that they attacked. Taking alternate swings at the timber, they were again aiming to cut it in two and complete the operation ahead of the other two teams. Chips of wood were flying in all directions as the commentator on the loud-speaker system urged the various axemen on.

'You just wouldn't believe *anybody* could swing an axe as fast – and accurately – as that if you hadn't seen it for yourself, would you?' Jo exclaimed. And Lee, who'd been thinking exactly the same, nodded.

The final feat that the men performed was easily the toughest as well as the most spectacular. Two substantial poles, each several metres high, were propped upright in the centre of the ring. An axeman advanced on each and rapidly cut into the trunk at about waist-height; then, when he'd made a satisfactory V-shaped incision he slipped a plank of wood into the aperture so that it projected outwards like the branch of a tree. Nimbly he then

73

leapt on to that branch and, using it as a scaffold, cut into the pole again in exactly the same way. Raining blows on the timber he carved himself another foothold – inserted a plank – and thus gradually ascended to the top of the pole! The first one to reach the summit was, of course, the winner.

The volley of cheering and the applause that rang round the arena when the axemen completed their performance was almost deafening.

'Wow, that really was something!' Lee said, still savouring the agility and strength of the artists with the axes. 'I'd no idea the show was going to be as good as this. What's next?'

'Come on,' said Joanne happily, seizing him by the hand. 'There's something I'd like you to see. Different from what you've just seen but . . .'

Lee didn't protest, even though he felt he was almost being dragged towards a marquee that bore the rather depressing word 'Handicrafts' on a board by its entrance. He couldn't imagine what on earth would interest her among tea-cosies and embroidered cushions and patterns of dried flowers. In fact, she led him to a section that had been turned into a small picture gallery. Paintings of all descriptions and standards hung against the canvas walls.

'Well, what do you think?' inquired Joanne, standing well back but staring fixedly at one row in particular.

'Well, what?' Lee was asking puzzledly until he

spotted a picture of a motor-cycle being ridden on what was plainly a motocross circuit. 'Oh, I see – yes, that's not bad at all.'

He went up to peer at it. 'Hey, Jo! Do you see, that's my number – it's – it's my bike! It's a painting of me right in the middle of the action.'

'Well done, Lee,' responded Joanne softly, breathing out in relief that he'd identified himself so quickly. She watched him read the label that was stuck temporarily to the frame.

'But – but, Jo, it's *your* picture!' he cried in genuine amazement, swinging round to face her. 'I didn't know you could paint like this. And to do a motocross picture of me. I think that's fantastic. It looks dead accurate. How did you manage that? You've hardly ever seen me racing.'

'Well, I see enough of bikes, don't I, so I just drew one. And it wasn't any problem to fit you on the bike, if you, er, see what I mean.'

Lee was now looking at a small blue sticker on the corner of the frame. 'Hey!' he said excitedly. 'You've actually won a prize as well! They've given you second prize. Terrific!' He paused and then asked, 'Is that why you wanted come here? Because you'd won a prize, I mean?'

'Hardly,' she answered. 'They didn't judge them until this morning. So I could only hope for the best that they'd accepted it for showing.'

'I don't know how you managed to keep quiet

75

about it for so long, Jo. I mean, if it had been mine, I'd have rushed over here as soon as we arrived and then told *everybody* about it.'

Joanne shook her head. 'No, you wouldn't, Lee. You're not the boastful type at all,' she told him. 'You're really quite good at a lot of things but you never let on to anybody if you can help it. I know – I'm a good observer, you see.'

Lee turned away and appeared to be taking a great interest in a painting of a fishing vessel unloading its catch. 'Er, I think I feel really hungry,' he announced. 'Do you know what I fancy? Fish and chips. I smelt them as we came past that take-away cabin – terrific.'

'O.K. I expect I could manage some, too. Seems ages since I had my breakfast. Look, I'll pay for them to celebrate – I get a whole £1 for second prize so we'll blow the lot on best quality Great Lingdale Show fish 'n' chips!'

'Thanks very much,' said Lee with genuine gratitude, 'but I think I should pay my share. I'm always getting free meals at your place and that's not fair, really. And Uncle Ken always seems to pile twice as much on my plate as he gives to Darren. I've tried to tell him not to but he won't listen.'

Jo, however, insisted that it was her day out; and so pay she did, for both of them. As they shuffled forward in the queue – for, in spite of the sunshine, everybody seemed to want to lunch off fish-and-chips – Joanne was silent for a time. Then, much to Lee's surprise, she asked him if he'd ever felt resentful when Darren received favourable treatment.

'How do you mean?' Lee asked. The question baffled him.

'Well, when there are just the two of you involved in something, it's Darren, isn't it, who gets first choice? You know, at motocross: first bike, first to get new equipment and spares, first in everything, really.'

Lee answered slowly, 'I hadn't really thought about it. But it's natural, I suppose, because he's older. Anyway, most people treat us alike – people that really know us, I mean, such as relatives.'

'No they don't,' said Joanne quickly. 'Dad, for one, doesn't treat you the same. That's why he always gives you extra helpings of food. He feels guilty because he shows Darren favouritism in everything else.'

'Oh, I just thought Uncle Ken felt I needed building up or something. I didn't think he had a personal motive like that – unless it was to use up some of the canned goods his firm sells!'

'Well, you can joke about it if you like, Lee, but I don't think it's fair.'

At that point they reached the head of the queue; and after they'd been served their mouths were too full of delicious cod to make conversation. Then, as they wandered towards the main show ring again, an announcement was made over the loudspeaker that the motor-cycle display would begin within the next five minutes.

'That's good timing,' said Lee, gulping down a chip that nearly seared his throat. 'Let's go and get a good position to watch from. I want to see if these guys are as good as the top scramblers.'

Afterwards, he was forced to admit that, in their own way, the German riders were incomparable. They rode as a team, cutting across each other's path on long diagonals with split-second timing at high speeds; they soared from ramps over each other's heads; they tore through colossal paper hoops simultaneously while travelling in opposite directions; and they even played a furious game of hockey ('a bit like polo on wheels,' as the commentator described it) in which the highlight was the feat of a goalkeeper who dribbled his way through the entire opposition to plant the ball in the net at the other end of the pitch.

'And now,' boomed the commentator, 'comes the chance for instant stardom for any youngster who has been thrilled by the superb riding we've all been watching. While the riders take a well-earned break before giving us their spectacular finale we're going to have a little competition.'

As he paused two men were wheeling out into the centre of the arena two junior-size motorcycles. All the metal-work had been painted in gleaming white. Several metres away two other men were measuring out distances from beneath the high point of a ramp and, at intervals, placing white tapes in straight lines on the turf.

'This is a competition,' the commentator resumed, 'in which the young rider can emulate the skills of our top riders. As you see, a ramp has been set up – but not *too* high! – for flying jumps on a bike. Any youngster under the age of fourteen is invited to have a go – and the one who makes the biggest leap will win a special prize.

'One thing I must say before you all rush forward to compete: every contestant *must* wear the helmet, the knee pads and the elbow pads that we are providing. We want heroes to step forward – but we don't want them to be damaged before they can claim the big prize!

'Right, then, young gentlemen – or even young *ladies*, come to that – who's going to be the first? Who's going to set the target everyone will have to beat?'

Joanne, eyes shining, turned to Lee. 'Well, *you're* going to have a go, aren't you? I mean, it's *made* for you.'

Lee hesitated. 'Oh, I don't know. It's a bit like – well – showing-off, isn't it, with a huge crowd like this?'

'Rubbish!' responded Joanne positively. 'If
79

you're doing something that comes quite naturally to you then it can't be – what do they call it? – oh yes, exhibitionism. Anyway, if you're not going to have a shot at winning, I am.'

'*You* are? But how can you? I mean, have you ever ridden a real motor-bike, Jo? It's not the easiest – '

'Of course I have, Lee! You don't think I *ignore* those two bikes at home, do you? They're available, so I ride 'em when I feel like it – and that's quite often. And now I feel like shooting off that ramp. After all, it's not very high, is it? I'd be pretty feeble if I couldn't manage that.'

A moment later, Lee, still somewhat non-plussed, was staring at her back as she advanced determinedly into the arena. She seemed to have been springing surprises on him all day. But the biggest of them was certainly the news that she had been riding the motocross bikes. Yet it was typical of her to react in such a positive way to something that caught her interest.

He followed her into the centre of the show ring.

The commentator, who was also in charge of the event, was delighted to welcome a girl as the first contestant – and he made a fuss of her. Joanne stood there quite imperturbably as he babbled on about her initiative and sense of adventure and, he was sure, her 'terrific skills as a dare-devil rider'! Lee, when he was briefly interviewed, made no reference

to the fact that he and Jo were cousins; as a result
of probing questions from the commentator, he
admitted that he took part in schoolboy scrambles
and had to suffer the consequences. The man with
the microphone tried to make out that Lee must be
'a champion *rough*-rider in the making'. He was
thankful when, after much cajolery, a few more
candidates emerged from the crowd around the
arena.

'I think that it should be ladies first,' announced
the commentator predictably. 'So Joanne here, our
leading lady, indeed our *only* lady competitor, is
going to be the one to set the target all the rest have
to aim at. I'm absolutely positive it's going to be a
terrific one. So, Jo – I'm sure that's what they call
you at home!– when the starter drops his hand, off
you go.'

Joanne, by now wearing helmet and protective
pads, had already been allowed to familiarise herself
with the bike by riding it round in circles while the
commentator was chatting to other contestants.
There had been a draw among the boys for places
in the line-up and the one to follow Joanne was
similarly warming up on the far side of the long
wooden ramp. Lee was to be the last but one to
ride.

Now, coming round in a great sweep and building up speed, Joanne lined up her approach to the
ramp. She looked, thought Lee, as if she'd spent

her life on the seat of a motor-cycle. No one would fault her style.

Up the ramp she roared, and through the air she soared, to touch down neatly and unwaveringly beyond the third tape. The crowd gave her a great cheer.

'What a fantastic performance by the little lady, Miss Joanne Wragby!' the commentator crowed ecstatically. 'That will really take some beating, folks. As I forecast, she could be a great winner: the *first* to have a go and the *first* at the finish.'

He'd forecast nothing of the kind but no one attempted to correct him. Everyone was watching the second rider zoom up the ramp. But he landed well short of Joanne's mark which was being indicated by a miniature yellow flag. The applause from the spectators, though, was still generous.

Lee, as he watched the others attempting to improve on Joanne's record, became increasingly nervous. He had a terrible fear that he was going to make a hash of his riding, that he would miss the ramp altogether or slide off it, sideways. He began to wish that he could get out of the arena without riding at all.

'O.K., son, your turn,' called one of the commentator's assistants to Lee. 'Time to get mounted.'

As he pulled on the helmet and the knee and elbow pads Lee suddenly recognised the man as

one of the star performers in the German display
team. He hadn't realised that they would bother to
help out in what was really a children's sideshow.

'Not nervous, are you, son?' the man suddenly
asked him. Lee, licking his lips, didn't know how
to answer. 'No need to be, son. All you've got to
do is enjoy yourself on this bike. Be confident! If
you're confident in yourself, then you can do anything you want to do. O.K.?'

'O.K.,' replied Lee with a grin that was the result
of a lot of effort.

'That's it, then! You look good on that bike –
look as though you know what it's all about. Ridden
before, have you?'

'Oh yes.'

'Thought so. You can always tell the tigers from the rabbits in this game. Right, away you go!'

Lee pulled away and began his sweep towards the starter. All at once, he felt at one with the bike. Next instant, he saw the starter's hand drop – and he raced towards the ramp.

Even as he took off, and experienced the thrill again of being airborne, he knew that his control of the bike was perfect; that his weight was in exactly the right place.

The touchdown, as far as he could tell, was also faultless and he felt a glow of triumph as the crowd roared its approval. As he wheeled away to return the bike to the organisers he saw that a yellow flag

was being planted a fraction ahead of the one marking Joanne's effort – and Joanne had still been in the lead when he made his jump.

'There you are, son, I told you everything would be great for you,' said the German rider as Lee handed over the bike. 'You see, all top people are a little nervous before they have to perform a special feat. That is a very good thing because it makes the adrenalin flow through the veins – and, zoom!, you give a better performance.'

'That was great!' Joanne enthused, giving him a hug. 'You've won, I reckon, because that lad riding now looks as though he might not even reach the top of the ramp!'

He did – but at such a speed that he had no chance at all of jumping beyond the first tape. The commentator himself led the applause for what he described as 'a brave try' and then announced the result of the competition:

'As you saw, ladies and gentlemen, two of the contestants finished well ahead of all the others. What's more, they finished so close together that we couldn't separate 'em! So the result is a dead heat – a dead heat between that plucky young lady, our very first rider, Miss Joanne Wragby, and the boy who would surely have won outright if it had been judged on style alone, Lee Parnaby. So, ladies and gentlemen, please give our super winners a big hand!'

Then, to their intense delight, he presented them with trophies: beautiful silver-plated models of the bikes they'd been riding. They were easily the best prizes Lee had ever seen.

'You know,' said Jo as they walked out of the arena together, 'I think they were a bit generous to me. You *should* have won outright, Lee. Still, I'm sure you will do at the next motocross after the way you rode today.'

Six

On the morning of the next meeting of the Skal-brooke Schoolboy Motorcycle Club it was Darren who was nearest to the telephone when it rang at his home. Because he was avidly reading a new motor-cycling magazine he didn't react for some moments; in any case, he was hoping that someone else would come along and answer it. Eventually, the caller's persistence broke down his resistance.

'Oh, hi, Joanne,' he said quite brightly when he recognised the voice. 'How are things with you?'

'Not so bad, Daz, but they're not going to be so good with you when you hear the news,' she told him briskly. 'Dad's not going to be able to take you and Lee and the bikes to the motocross today. He's had to – '

'What!' Darren screeched. 'He's got to! I'm all set for a great ride today, for a big win – I know it. He can't let us down like this, Joanne.'

'He didn't have any alternative. One of his salesmen has got into some sort of trouble and Dad had to go up to Newcastle last night to sort things out. Dad's the only one who could do it. There's no chance he'll be back home before Tuesday night, he told Mum. So – '

'O.K., so what about Aunt Sue? *She* can take us instead. She won't be much good at fixing the bikes but she can still drive us there – that's the main thing.'

'Sorry, no chance of that, either. You see, Dad – '

'*Somebody's* got to get us there!' Darren exploded. 'I just *can't* miss this meeting after having such rotten luck last time when that crazy idiot Nicholson knocked me off the bike. I *must* race today!'

'I expect Lee feels the same,' Joanne retorted coolly. 'Look, Daz, I think I'd better talk to him so that we can sort things out. He'll come up with some *useful* ideas.'

It seemed at first as if Darren were going to protest; but, perhaps thinking better of it, he put the phone down and went to yell for his brother. It didn't take him long to find him; Lee was helping to prepare a picnic lunch for all of them.

'It's a disaster!' Darren declared. 'Uncle Ken's let us down. So see what you can come up with, Lee.'

There were no futile interruptions from Lee as

89

Joanne explained that her father had been obliged to use the van to get to Newcastle because his company car was unluckily off the road for a few days; thus there was no vehicle that her mother could use.

'Dad did everything he could to get somebody else to take you and the bikes. He rang dozens of people, but no luck at all. They were all pretty sympathetic but just couldn't help. So it's pretty hopeless, Lee, unless *you* know somebody with the right sort of transport – and somebody who'd be willing to turn out on a Sunday. I know how much you've been looking forward to competing again – and Dad said to tell you how sorry he felt.'

As she talked Lee's mind was racing round all the names he could think of: people who might assist in a crisis. Unfortunately, his total didn't rise above four and each of them he had to discount for one reason or another.

Daz was tugging at his sleeve, desperate to know what was being decided.

'Come on, wonder brother,' he was saying between clenched teeth. 'You're supposed to be a genius at sorting out big problems.'

'Shut up a minute, Daz,' Lee told him. 'This isn't as simple as collecting your lost property off the chapel roof.'

To Lee's surprise, that did silence him. With Joanne, he resumed a discussion of possibilities

90

until it was agreed that every one was an impossibility. So few people possessed a trailer or a van. Except ...

'Hey, Jo, I've just thought of somebody!' he said excitedly. 'He's not *exactly* a mate of mine but he's always very friendly and seems to like me. Got just the right transport for us, too. Big old grocery van – bags of room if he removes the shelves.'

'Who's that, then?'

'Oh, Mr Thirlwell. He's the travelling greengrocer that comes round here – has been doing for years. His van's almost *prehistoric* but he looks after it like a – like a family pet. He lives not so far from here so it would be easy to get to see him. I'll get off now.'

'Would it help, Lee, if I came as well? I mean, perhaps I could help in some way – or just help to persuade him. If you tell me where it is I'll meet you there – won't take long on my push-bike. Could be that two heads are better than one – that's what Mum always says.'

Lee agreed and explained how to get to Mr Thirlwell's. Then he rang off and told his anxious brother what he had in mind. Darren, predictably, didn't think much of the idea. It seemed that he hadn't a high opinion of the greengrocer, though he admitted he'd never actually talked to him.

'Have you a better suggestion?' Lee asked as he hurried to the door.

'Er, no.'

'Thought not,' Lee flung back over his shoulder.

He was in luck. Mr Thirlwell was at home, relaxing with a Sunday newspaper, following, as he put it, a hearty breakfast.

'Well, this is a pleasure, Lee – and a most unexpected one,' the greengrocer greeted him, beamingly. 'You've run out of vitamins, haven't you? That's what you've come for, isn't it?'

'Not, er, exactly, Mr Thirlwell. I want to borrow your van.'

To Lee's surprise, the greengrocer didn't even blink; and his smile didn't fade. 'Ah, is that it? Well, now, what use do you have in mind for it?'

'To transport motor-bikes – mine and my brother Darren's – to the motocross club meeting. It's today, you see, and Uncle Ken, who usually takes us, well, he – '

Before he could get any further the front door bell rang; and, guiltily, Lee guessed who it would be. Until that moment he'd forgotten he should have waited outside the house for Joanne to arrive. Mr Thirlwell peered through the bay window and remarked that it appeared to be his day for receiving young visitors.

Hastily, Lee explained, as Mr Thirlwell let her in, that Joanne was his cousin and that it was her father who normally attended to all their travel and riding arrangements. Patiently, the greengrocer listened to the entire story from the two of them without interrupting once.

'Fascinating!' he pronounced when they finished. 'I'd no idea that this scrambling business was so highly organised – or that all you youngsters were involved. I've always like motor-cycles because in my Army days I used to ride one, most of the time. I was in the Royal Signals and they're the real experts at that game – their motor-cycle displays at the big tournaments were always the highlight. Oh, yes!

'Still, I mustn't bore you with my reminiscing. Time mustn't be lost. So, let's get off to the garage and see to the van.'

Lee was quite stunned. 'You mean, you *will* help us?'

'Of course, young Lee! What are friends for but to help when the need arises?'

As they followed Mr Thirlwell to the garage at the bottom of a long, narrow garden Lee and Joanne exchanged delighted whispers.

'I never imagined it would be so *easy*.'

'Tell you what, Daz is going to get a shock when we turn up with the bikes surrounded by apples and oranges and spuds!'

In fact, somewhat to their disappointment, the ancient van was almost empty. Mr Thirlwell explained that, instead of making his rounds on a Monday, he went off to the wholesale market to replenish his supplies for the first half of the week. They helped him to remove various crates and sacks and some of the shelves; the one item they were asked to treat with great reverence was the pair of old-fashioned ('but wonderfully accurate – just as good as your new-fangled computer') brass weighing scales.

'There, I think that'll give you all the room you need for a couple of bikes,' Mr Thirlwell said. 'So hop in the front with me and give me directions to your home, Joanne. I must say, I'm quite looking forward to this race meeting of yours. It's going to seem quite like old times for me to be surrounded by motor-cycles – and to sniff that most distinctive of smells, the mixture of petrol and oil. Lovely!'

Almost as if the racing spirit had suddenly got into his blood, he drove the van at a rattling rate; yet he still found time to wave to favoured customers he spotted in their gardens or out walking. Some of them displayed astonishment at seeing him driving his van on a Sunday morning – and at such speed.

Aunt Sue took their arrival in a greengrocer's van in her stride and watched with interest as the racing bikes were propelled up a makeshift ramp and then secured for the journey to the Autodrome.

They were climbing back into the cab when Joanne's mother put her hand on Lee's shoulder as if to detain him.

'There isn't anything you've forgotten, is there, Lee?' she inquired.

Lee frowned and thought hard. Eventually, still puzzled, he had to admit that he couldn't think of anything they'd overlooked.

'How about,' asked his aunt with a grin, 'your ... *brother?*'

'Oh, murder! Daz! I *had* forgotten him. But, you see, he didn't think we'd find any transport. So ... Still, we'll just have to go and pick him up and – '

'No, don't worry, Lee,' Aunt Sue said quickly, still smiling. 'All's well. Darren has been on the phone to me – trust him! – to say he's making his own way to the Autodrome and that he'll meet you there – if, as he put it, you manage to find a jet-propelled horse-and-cart. I rather gathered that he was hoping to borrow a bike from somebody.'

'He would! I'll bet he didn't think of trying to borrow a bike for me. Typical of him to think only of himself. Still, he'll get a bit of a shock when we roll up with our own bikes in this terrific transporter!'

'Only,' pointed out the driver of the transporter in a surprisingly firm voice, 'if we get a move on *now.*'

Seven

In the paddock the greatest amount of attention was being paid to the Shearsmith Special. Relays of parents and fellow competitors kept coming up to admire the gleaming black machine but none of them could extract any of its technical secrets from Greg or his father, although they weren't denying that the bike's exhaust system was, as Mr Shearsmith put it, 'where it all happens.' One of the marshals who'd been to look at it had another view. 'Maybe it does all happen down there,' he muttered to a friend, 'but in the final analysis everything depends on the skills of the rider – and young Greg'll need to learn how to control himself during a race before he gets the best out of that bike. And after being suspended I reckon he'll be riding in a crazier fashion than ever.'

Greg's confidence – already as high as the clouds on a gloriously sunny day – had received a boost when he learned that, for this meeting,

96

they'd be going round the circuit in the opposite direction.

'That's bound to give you and me a big advantage,' he chortled to Lee when they met a few minutes after the arrival of Mr Thirlwell's van. 'All the other riders will have to adjust to the new course after the last meeting. But as we didn't race then we won't have to think about what happened last time. We'll make a flying start while they're still working out which way to go!'

Lee wasn't at all convinced by that argument but he didn't say so. He wasn't going to do anything to jeopardize the offer of help he and Darren had received from Greg's father.

Mr Shearsmith had come across to them as soon as they'd begun to unload the bikes in the car park. Initially, he wanted to say how much appreciation he had for Lee's loyalty at the time of the suspension because, he said, it would have been so easy for Lee to protest that Greg had led him astray; instead, Lee, in Mr Shearsmith's words, had 'acted and taken your punishment like a man – without a whimper.' Now, when he discovered that the brothers' uncle was unable to be present, he had volunteered his services as mechanic and general assistant. The offer was accepted with alacrity by Lee; they needed somebody to tune and, if necessary, service their bikes because he'd already discovered that, helpful though Mr Thirlwell wanted

to be, his knowledge of modern motocross machines was virtually nil.

'I'll keep you in top racing condition,' Mr
Shearsmith promised, 'even if it means that you
beat Greg to the chequered flag in the process!'

Darren, when he arrived a few minutes later,
actually managed to sound grateful for once for the
arrangements Lee had made on his behalf. He'd
caught a bus from home into town. Then he was
lucky enough to get a lift to the Autodrome from
the parents of a club member who'd been filling up
with petrol at a self-service station near the bus
stop. Darren admitted that he'd been worrying
about who would attend to their bikes in Uncle
Ken's absence if his brother did succeed in getting
them delivered to the track.

'But I didn't think you'd do it,' he told Lee; and
then added in typical fashion, 'I assumed it was
going to be another desperately unlucky day for me
- for us, I mean.'

Joanne and Lee exchanged a laugh about that
remark as soon as they were out of earshot. While
Darren remained in the paddock to discuss tactics
and performances with his cronies, his brother and
cousin decided to walk the circuit and watch the
cadets, the youngest riders, in action in the first
scramble of the day. Inevitably, they found themselves rivetted by events at V-One, the most acute
of the severe bends on the oval-shaped course. Far

too many of the riders seemed unable to judge the speed at which they could hope to negotiate it – and so bikes and bodies were catapulting in several directions.

'I just hope you're not going to go the same way!' Joanne said to Lee as she helped to lift one tiny boy to his feet and then reunited-him with his bike. Although the rider was seven years old he looked much younger.

'Don't worry, I've worked out just what's right for this corner,' Lee assured her. 'I doubt, though, that Greg has. In these fast conditions I reckon there'll be an almighty pile-up here if Greg gets himself in the leading group – and I don't see where else *he* will be!'

'This dip into the bend is going to make it even more difficult. It'd be mad to come down into this at anything more than – what? – third gear?'

He grinned. 'One thing's definite – if you arrive here flat out, that's where you'll finish: flat out on your back on a stretcher. Have you noticed how many St John ambulancemen are stationed here?'

It was also the place for overhearing hard-luck stories related by other spectators. The most amazing one concerned the rider whose bike simply snapped in two, with the rear half flying across the track and knocking another competitor from his machine. Joanne shuddered when she heard that one.

Silently and thoughtfully, Joanne and Lee made their way back towards the paddock while the cadets were on their final circuit. The Juniors would be racing before Lee went out to ride but he wanted to check over his bike again and perhaps have a word with Mr Shearsmith. But they paused as one rider swerved recklessly across the track and very nearly charged through the marker tapes alongside them.

At least one spectator was quite unmoved by that dangerous manœuvre. At that moment he was telling his companion earnestly, 'You know, my Dad will brain me if I don't get a high place today. He says if I don't start improving rapidly everyone will know he's got an *idiot* for a son!'

Joanne's eyebrows shot up. Then she whispered to Lee: 'Well, at least you don't have *that* sort of pressure to put up with, do you?'

'No,' Lee agreed, 'but I do have a mad brother to cope with! And you never know what he's going to do next. He'll be desperate to win today to get even with Graham Relton. He really does hate Graham and I don't think he could stand another failure if Graham wins.'

'But he's not going to win, is he, Lee? It's *your* turn today for the chequered flag.'

'Oh, come on, Jo,' Lee replied lightly, 'I'll need a heck of a lot of luck to overtake Gray Relton if he's really in top form. He's easily the best in our age group and he's got a great machine. So I reckon – '

He stopped as, without warning, Joanne dashed away. For a moment, he thought he'd said something to offend her, though he couldn't imagine what it was. Then he saw that she was making for one of the market stalls where people were selling riders' clothing and equipment and even such oddities as woolly toys (presumably to tempt parents with young children complaining that they were being neglected).

Before Lee could reach her Joanne had made a purchase and was coming back towards him.

'There you are!' she said triumphantly. 'That should bring you all the luck you need. The rest of the race depends on your determination, Lee. I think you've got all the skill you need.'

She handed him a key-ring with the glossy black leather tab cleverly cut into the shape of a cat.

'Thanks, Jo,' was all he could think of saying. Then, noting the expression on her face, he added, 'I'll carry it with me always. And I'll put every key I get on it.'

He was still fingering the key-ring in his trouser pocket when they returned to the paddock. Practically the first person he saw was Darren, strutting almost possessively between the rows of bikes in company with one of his cronies. It was obvious that Daz had found someone to attend to his own

101

machine. By now, Lee surmised, his brother would have convinced himself that it was his own idea to travel to the meeting in Mr Thirlwell's spectacular van. Certainly Daz appeared to be in a confident mood.

'It's in beautiful condition, isn't it?' Lee remarked as he trailed his fingers lightly over the frame of his green-and-silver motor-cycle. He'd already had a practice ride round the circuit but he was wishing that he could go out again before the race started.

'Well, it should be, considering all the hours that Dad spends on it every week,' Jo was saying. 'He wouldn't devote any more time to it if it were my bike, I reckon. One of these days someone is going to show him that girls can tackle motocross just as well as boys ...'

Lee wasn't really listening to her. The announcement was being made that the riders in the Intermediates' race should move towards the starting gate. The butterflies in his stomach fluttered with the abandon of the pennants above the riders' helmets when the throttles opened up. He glanced across at his brother, who had drawn a place almost alongside the starter, but Darren was staring fixedly ahead. Like every other rider, he knew that a flying start was essential.

One of the spectators was suddenly calling attention to the plight of a boy whose engine had cut out. The bike was wheeled out of the line and frantic efforts were made by the lad's father to restore power. Anxiously, other riders fiddled with helmet straps or goggles or just prayed that the starter would get on with his job. Every second of waiting was an extra burden on the nervous system. For many of the contestants, it wasn't only the warmth of the day that was causing them to sweat so freely.

The starter's knuckles whitened – and, next instant, the tape concertinaed across the track.

The scramble was on!

As the field spurted away, Lee felt a sharp blow on his right leg which very nearly caused him to collide with the bike on his left. He had been struck into by the rider of a very battered-looking Yamaha who seemed unable to control his machine. Lee couldn't identify the boy under his dusty helmet.

Already he had lost ground as a result of his instinctive swerve away from the Yamaha. But as soon as he engaged a higher gear he sensed that his bike was in top racing condition. Just what Mr Shearsmith had done to it he had no idea; but the engine note was a perfect melody.

By the first S-bend, Graham Relton had established a useful lead with the bounding Greg Shearsmith in second place. Lee, breaking away from the tail-enders, was able to see that Darren was not among the leading group as, briefly, the pace-setters came back towards him. Then they hurtled away again in the direction of the first of the major hazards: V-Two.

As the riders went into the next, and well-banked, bend, marshals were already shouting warnings to cut down on speed. The race was being run at an electrifying rate with Greg snapping at Graham's rear wheel. He was putting on all the power he possessed in order to overtake the leader. Yet they were not drawing far ahead of the pack behind them. In these fast conditions everyone seemed to believe he could set up a personal lap record.

Lee, now weaving his way through to the middle of the field, edged forward on his bike as he approached V-Two. For such a severe bend the rider's balance had to be absolutely correct.

Then, just as he decided on his line of navigation, a Suzuki slithered perilously right across his path from the left. Lee hadn't even been aware that the rider was so close to him; but the boy had lost control in the ultra-fast racing conditions while in too high a gear.

Deftly, Lee changed down again even as he steered sharply to his left, and then regained his chosen course with another flick of his wrists. Now he had enough momentum to carry him round the corner at what had to be maximum speed for the day. As he completed the switch-back he saw that the Suzuki rider was being helped to his feet by ambulance attendants.

That near-scrape, and the way he had avoided trouble, set the adrenalin flowing again and also gave a great boost to his confidence. He began to believe that this could be his day after all. Moments later he was blasting superbly over a jump and landing with immense style; so much so that he won a spontaneous round of applause from hardened spectators more used to cheering on only their own sons and daughters.

With only half a lap completed he had overtaken half-a-dozen riders and was now among the main pack – and no more than a couple of lengths adrift of his brother. As usual, Darren's black-and-yellow striped helmet was easily picked out; but, for some reason, the self-styled 'Tiger of the Track' was not competing with his customary snarling endeavour. He had allowed the cut-throat leaders, Gray Relton and Greg Shearsmith, to pounce into a clear lead. Those two were having a battle all to themselves as they scorched into V-One, the toughest test on the entire track.

They went into it side by side, neither willing to concede so much as a centimetre in room or deviate a fraction off the chosen route to success. Inevitably, they touched – and it was Greg's glossy black machine that went careering off course. Graham, slim and slightly built and fragile in appearance, was really as strong as whipcord; in a physical contest, he'd rarely come off second best. He wasn't going to now, either.

Greg, trying desperately to correct his deflection, overdid it. Unwilling to lose even a single rev, he tried to keep up with his rival – and paid the predictable penalty. He was catapulted from the jack-knifing Special and soared over the perimeter tape to land in a heap among the scattering spectators.

Graham, displaying no emotion at all behind his dust-free goggles, roared on into a clear lead. At that moment, he had every reason to assume that he was on course for another triumph.

With the help of by-standers and an alarmed ambulanceman, Greg was quickly on his feet and assuring everyone that he was still in good shape and determined to get back into the race. His father had sprinted across to scrutinize the Special and ensure that it had suffered no major damage. Then, with a command to Greg to 'Stick to it!' Mr Shearsmith pushed him back on to the bike and into the race. Before the nearest marshal could blink a second time, Greg was speeding away.

Nonetheless, he had lost more than a share of the lead. Several of the riders who had been trying to break away from the pack behind Relton and Shearsmith at last succeeded after rounding V-One. Darren Parnaby, inspired by the sight of Greg's dramatic departure from the track, made

the most positive charge. After his earlier worries, he was beginning to get over the absence of Uncle Ken, who had always given him so much encouragement. Daz was no longer looking out for him and his signals at crucial stages of a race. This time he was on his own and would have to ride his own race. On the brief straight he engaged top gear – and in an instant he seemed to be flying.

Lee, too, judged that it was time to increase his own pace. V-One proved to be a less daunting obstacle than he'd supposed. He sensed now that he was riding near the top of his form – and the sight of Darren's helmet, bobbing just ahead of him, was an additional spur. But he wanted to pick precisely the right moment to sweep past his brother.

So, after sniping his way through the field, Lee was lying in fifth position at the end of the first of the four laps. Graham Relton possessed such a substantial lead that some spectators were talking about the only race being the one for second place.

One man, though, who hadn't written off his son's chances of victory was Harry Shearsmith. Darting across the oval, from vantage point to vantage point, he was urging Greg to greater efforts – and Greg, being Greg, was responding as best he could. Before another circuit had been completed he was again among the challengers – and by now Darren was in second place, only just in front of his younger brother. Lee felt that he could 'take' Daz whenever he wanted to but he was biding his time. His machine was responding beautifully to every demand he made of it ... and he knew that he had plenty of power in reserve.

'Just look at that kid on the black bike!' one spectator was yelling to another. 'He's really the wild one. If only he'd settle down he could be a world-beater. He's been on the floor once and now he's battling for second place again – but look at the way he's riding. He's all over the place!'

Greg had realised only a split-second before the man spoke that something was wrong with his steering. But the fault, he was certain, would rapidly correct itself – nothing went wrong with a bike his father serviced. Having carved his way back into a springboard position, Greg wasn't going to drop back for any reason.

At that moment, Lee decided to deliver the telling thrust and accelerate past Darren. All three riders were in one of the narrowest sections of the track, with shallow banking on both sides of the slight downhill gradient. Lee wanted his brother to *know* exactly who had relegated him to third place.

Lee aimed to burst past on Darren's left. With a right-hander coming up, Daz wouldn't expect to be challenged on that side. So the element of surprise would also be in Lee's favour.

He moved out – and then surged forward. Momentarily, the bikes were level. Daz, glancing sideways, was startled to see that it was his brother.Briefly, his control wavered; the bikes came together, the boys' knees touched. Then, instinctively, Daz steered to the right. In the moment that they parted Greg pounced with the intention of driving through the gap between them.

It was then that the steering on the Shearsmith Special let him down. The erratic course he'd been following had actually been forced on him by the looseness of the handlebars, damaged when he crashed. In his eagerness to get Greg back into the race Harry Shearsmith had failed to spot the defect.

Greg, unable to manœuvre his machine, banged

fiercely into the rival on his right. Darren was flung into the banking; and from there he slid in a sitting position to the ground, an expression of astonishment rather than pain visible beneath his goggles. The Special wobbled precariously back and forth across the track for several lengths before it, too, collapsed.

By then, Lee, miraculously unaffected by the earlier touch from Daz's bike, was clear of all trouble. In one fell swoop two of his deadliest rivals were out of the race. Now he was in second place with his nearest pursuer almost fifty metres behind him.

'Go *on*, Lee, you can do it!' someone yelled to him – and one glance at the slim figure beside the track told him that it was Joanne. She had seen that there was nothing for him to worry about now as long as he had the speed to catch Graham Relton.

Lee was optimistic. He knew that his luck was in, just as Darren's was out. For once, his brother's inevitable claim that he'd been the victim of bad luck would be justified. Lee thought of the black cat key-ring in his pocket – and powered on.

His style on the straights, as he positioned himself on the bike to keep the front wheel skipping over the bumps at maximum speed, drew cheers from the spectators. Metre by metre he closed the gap between himself and the leader.

Graham, suddenly made aware by the screeching of his fans that he had a challenger, risked a backward glance just as he approached V-One for the last time. As his concentration momentarily faltered, so did his control of the bike. The wobble was enough for him to lose his momentum.

Exultantly, Lee seized his chance to storm into the lead on the final, crucial corner in a flurry of dust.

As the flag fell and he zipped across the finishing line, two lengths ahead of Graham Relton, his arms went up in sheer delight.

'That was wonderful, Lee, really wonderful,' Joanne greeted him as he swept into the paddock.

'I just wish Dad had been here to see you win your first motocross.'

'I didn't need him, Jo. It was you who brought me luck – you and your black cat.'

'Rubbish!' she said, trying not to blush. 'You didn't need luck. You won because you were good enough to win and because you *wanted* to win. Most of all, because you believed you could win. That counts more than luck.'

Lee grinned. 'If you say so,' he told her.

MICHAEL HARDCASTLE

Fast From the Gate

One

As the sharp left-hand corner came up, Lee Parnaby shifted a trifle nervously in the seat of his bike but didn't reduce the revs. This time, he was determined to take it at maximum speed to set himself up for the downhill jump. His green-and-silver machine, freshly tuned, was responding beautifully. It had, he felt, never been better. So, this time, it was his own nerve, not the bike's performance, that was being put to the test.

Delicately his fingers played the throttle as he positioned the bike for the turn. Then, tilting, stabbing down with his left foot, trailing it over the loose earth, he was through the angle and racing towards the most fearsome hazard on the Skalbrooke Schoolboy Motorcycle Club's circuit. It was an approach he'd made hundreds of times in the past couple of years. But never had he approached it at the speed he was doing now.

Suddenly, his mouth went utterly dry. His

tongue felt huge. After all, the last time he'd attempted a very fast downhill jump he'd crashed. And that was only ten minutes ago, as he couldn't help remembering. His weight, he'd since worked out, had been in the wrong place on landing. He'd been too far forward and the front wheel came down first, spilling him helplessly across the track. Amazingly, though, he'd done no damage to himself or the bike. Perhaps, that time, he'd just been lucky. . . .

Instinctively now, he re-distributed his weight towards the rear. The trees clutching the hillside below seemed to tilt at him as the ground fell away. On the rim of the hill, it would disappear completely beneath him. His fingers tightened their grip.

He went into the take-off full-bore, hauling back on the handle-bars with all his strength as if trying to drag the whole bike into his chest. Like an Olympic downhill ski-jumper, he was shooting out into the unknown, striving desperately to make the perfect, balanced landing necessary to stay in the competition. To land – and still be running; that's what mattered.

The thump as the rear wheel banged down on unyielding stone jarred his entire body. Momentarily, the machine wavered. Then, closing down the throttle in order to brake effectively, he had control again. He'd done it!

118

Lee yelled his success to the world, though no one actually heard him. Like quicksilver, he flowed into the next bend; and the line he took was the perfect racing line. He hadn't had to think about it. His instincts as a scrambles rider had worked it out for him like a computer.

It was the fourth time in no more than about twenty minutes that he'd tackled that jump at high speed – and the first time he'd brought it off successfully. He wouldn't claim he'd mastered it but at least he knew he was coping with it in the right way. Never again would it terrify him, however fast he was going on take-off.

A downhill jump, Lee decided as he turned off the track to take a short cut back to the paddock area, was simply there to encourage a *winning* rider to win more convincingly.

He stood on the footrests, guiding the bike with infinite caution round a couple of bushes like a trials rider, and then increased the pace to bounce happily over a ribbed section to rejoin the main circuit. All evening he'd been refining his skills as a scrambler, working systematically in areas where he knew there was room for improvement. It was the start of a new season and Lee was determined to build on his success of the previous year. He'd won Intermediate races for the first time and established himself as one of the leading riders in his age-group in the Club. His ambitions were increasing all the time. At present, his chief aim was to gain selection for Skalbrooke's team for the Inter-Club races over the next few months.

The almost deserted paddock area was in sight when Lee spotted his cousin, Joanne Wragby, heading towards him. With her shoulder-length auburn hair streaming behind her and wearing her favourite rainbow-patterned sweater, she wasn't hard to recognise even from a distance. She wasn't so much running as making a connected series of successive long-jumps. Lee, who was exceedingly fond of his cousin, even though he didn't always show it, grinned behind his visor. The manner of Joanne's progress seemed to reflect her enthusiasms. It was her father, Ken Wragby, who'd introduced Lee and his brother Darren to motocross and provided them with their first bikes. He'd assumed that Joanne, because she was a girl, wouldn't be the slightest bit interested in such mechanised sport. That was quite wrong. Joanne, having grown up with bikes, had developed a great interest in them. Once she'd proved to her father that she was a perfectly capable rider, too, he'd promised her a bike of her own. She was due to receive it on her next birthday in July.

'Well, how did it go?' she demanded to know as Lee did a deliberately spectacular skid and came to a halt beside her. 'I hope you weren't doing all this show-off stuff out there on the track?'

'Nobody out there to see it – I hope. To be honest, I came off a couple of times when I really powered into that downhill jump. Then the first time I stayed on board after the jump I nearly came off again after landing because the bike was weaving about like a mad horse! I think I didn't come down early enough on the back wheel.'

'But you got it right in the end, Lee?'

'Er, just about, I think. Took off like a rocket – and kept going like a champion hare.'

'You've pinched that description from my essay for the school magazine!' she retorted accusingly. 'But it wasn't a rocket – that's too obvious. It was an intergalactic missile.'

'Couldn't pronounce that!' Lee confessed, trying not to laugh. 'Anyway, it felt terrific when I did it the last time so that must mean it works. I reckon even the Mad Motocrosser himself couldn't have done better – *and* stayed upright on two wheels.'

'Ah, talking of Greg Shearsmith, I think we'd better hurry up, Lee. He and his Dad want to get off home. They sent me out to see if you were on the way back.'

'O.K. Want to hop up on the back for a free ride to the pits?'

'What do you think I came all this way for?'

With alacrity she slid on to the long saddle and then clasped her hands behind her back instead of putting her arms round the driver. Lee, as he'd

121

once told her, felt 'hemmed in' when anybody did that.

By now the light on this evening of early spring was fading quickly, as mist from the estuary swirled inland. Because he'd been so absorbed by his private practice session Lee hadn't realised how late it was. He hoped Harry Shearsmith, Greg's father, wasn't going to complain that Lee had delayed their departure. In recent weeks Lee had come to rely heavily on Mr Shearsmith's generosity in transporting him and his bike to and from the Skalbrooke Club's circuits. Lee's father was in the Merchant Navy and thus mostly away from home.

Mr Shearsmith already had the engine of his expensive new minibus running when Lee, having accelerated over the final stretch and through the paddock area, reached the car park. He seemed calm enough but Greg was plainly angry even before he said a word.

'Did you fall off and knock yourself out?' he asked scathingly. 'We've been waiting ages for you, Lee. And I *told* you I wanted to get home in time to see that "Profile of a Boxer" programme. Probably miss half of it by the time we get there *now*.'

'Sorry,' Lee mumbled, feeling genuinely contrite. 'I just wasn't thinking about the time.'

Silently Mr Shearsmith propelled Lee's bike up the ramp and into the van. Carefully he secured it in the travelling frame alongside the black and gleaming Shearsmith Special, custom-built by himself. Greg's father was not only a very clever mechanic but a man with a talent for making money with all sorts of enterprises.

'Practice go well, did it son?' he asked Lee as he settled himself behind the wheel.

'Well, not bad in the end. I was trying to improve my, er, style on downhill jumps. I fell off a couple of times but I think I'd sorted things out by the time I packed it in.'

'I never think about changing *my* style for different bits of the course,' Greg announced from the front seat. 'Soon as I see daylight ahead of me I go flat out to win. Only way to ride a race, in my opinion.'

'So I'd noticed,' was Lee's quiet comment as he exchanged a knowing look with Joanne.

'Well, I've won as many scrambles as you, Lee Parnaby – and put up some of the fastest times on record,' Greg, whose hearing was acute, added.

Lee couldn't deny it. There were times when he couldn't help admiring Greg's fear-naught-and-stop-at-nothing approach to a motocross. Young Shearsmith really would go full speed into any danger spot without regard to the possible consequences. It took a certain degree of cold-blooded courage to do that. On the other hand, he certainly didn't care for Greg's sometimes totally ruthless attitude towards his fellow riders. It wasn't un-

123

known for him to knock other competitors out of his way when he saw, or thought he saw, an opening. He'd caused several spills in the pack in his time and been suspended for reckless riding. Greg had a high opinion of his own skills but he never failed to mention how much he owed to his father's 'wizardry with the spanners,' as he put it. Without any doubt, the Shearsmith Special, with its novel spread-of-power exhaust system, really was a marvellous machine.

Lee himself was grateful to Mr Shearsmith, who had provided both transport and tuning services when Lee had needed them for a club meeting the previous season. That was really the start of his friendship – if that's what it was – with Greg. He had the impression that, for some unexplained reason, Mr Shearsmith rather liked him and wanted to help him whenever help was needed. Yet Lee believed that he himself was different in almost every way from Harry Shearsmith's own son.

Now it was Mr Shearsmith who deftly turned the conversation to the subject of the first round of the Inter-Club Championship. It was his view that the selectors on the Skalbrooke Committee would have to pick both Greg and Lee for the Intermediates' team. Lee tried to suppress a grin when he realised that Mr Shearsmith wasn't including his brother, Darren, among the leading candidates. But then, Darren hadn't made much progress in the past year.

124

'Come on, Dad, step on it!' Greg urged as the minibus hovered on the tail of a rather lumbering saloon. 'I don't want to miss any *more* of that programme! I want to see the way Charlie McQuade knocked out that giant Italian. In the preview they said there'd be a terrific slow-motion replay.'

'I'm doing my best, son. No point in taking risks on a narrow, winding road like this.'

'Look, Mr Shearsmith, you don't have to take us right to my house – I mean, I know it's a big detour for you,' Lee suggested. 'If you drop us at top end of Lingdale Village we can easily wheel the bike home from there. We can take the short cut through Terson's Fields and that new estate.'

Harry Shearsmith hesitated for a moment or two before he made any reply; and in that interval he shot a sideways glance at his son. Lee had been aware for some time that Mr Shearsmith gave in rather easily when Greg wanted something. So he had no doubt at all that Mr Shearsmith would take the opportunity to shorten his journey. Still, that was only fair, in Lee's opinion.

'Well, if you really don't mind, Lee,' was the predictable comment. 'Certainly it would help us.'

So, after steering a neat course to avoid some boisterous revellers spilling from the pavement outside The Dog and Partridge Inn, he pulled up

125

on the broad parking area outside St Alban's, Lingdale's famous church-on-a-mound.

'Lucky for him I didn't knock one of those lads down,' remarked Mr Shearsmith, glancing back towards the pub as he unmoored Lee's motorcycle. 'He came so close he must have very nearly brushed against the van. Expect it's a party of young farmers celebrating something or other. It's their favourite pub.'

Lee took charge of the bike as soon as it touched the road and thanked him for his kindness.

'Sure you'll be all right on your own, then, Lee?' he asked anxiously if a trifle belatedly.

'Of course! In any case, I'm not on my own, am I? I told you, Joanne's staying with us this weekend while Uncle Ken and Aunt Sue are away in Paris. So she can do her share of pushing the old bike across the fields, can't you, Jo?'

'If you say so, Master,' she replied in a servile manner that made Mr Shearsmith laugh quite loudly.

'Right, then, we'll get off,' he said, slamming the door of the van. 'I'll pick you up at the usual time on Sunday for the club meeting. So long then – and take care.'

'You know, nobody would see us if we rode the bike across Terson's Fields,' Lee suggested. 'It'll be a real slog pushing it all the way. *And* it'll take ages.'

126

'Well, it's your own fault, Lee,' Jo pointed out. 'You were the keen one who told him to drop us off a thousand miles from home. You deserve to suffer. But you'll suffer a lot more if the police spot you riding a scrambles bike in the dark on public land. They'd probably never let you ride again, anywhere.'

Lee was just steering the bike into a narrow passageway that would lead them away from the houses when the front door of the end cottage was flung open. A woman dashed down the flagged pathway towards them. A street lamp was bracketed to the corner of the cottage at first floor level. By its light Lee recognised the old lady as Mrs Widdowson, who had a reputation as a witch-like eccentric. He'd never have believed she could move so fast if he hadn't seen her.

'Young man, you're just what I need to deal with a terrible problem in my fruit bushes!' she called to Lee. He was still startled by her appearance and didn't know what to answer; but Joanne instantly had a fit of giggles.

'It's *not* a laughing matter, young lady!' Mrs Widdowson thundered, sternness replacing her agitation. 'You wouldn't be laughing if a stupid donkey was *devouring* your livelihood. It's eating up every one of my lovely fruit bushes. We've got to put a stop to it at once. I need your help.'

'A donkey?' Lee had concluded that she really

was as crazy as most of the villagers believed. 'But where's it come from? I mean, are you *sure* it's a donkey in your garden?'

'Oh, don't take my word for it,' she retorted witheringly. 'Come and see it for yourself. But hurry, hurry. I've lost enough bushes already.'

Propping the bike carefully against the gatepost, Lee ran down the path in the wake of the sprightly Mrs Widdowson and Joanne, straight through the long, narrow cottage and into the narrow and even longer back garden. True enough, a donkey was there, chewing contentedly on a bush. As they arrived beside it, the donkey eyed them carefully but not for a second did it stop eating. Its long ears moved back and forth like signalling flags as Mrs Widdowson explained that the beast, as she was now calling it, had already demolished most of the gooseberries and was now attacking the blackcurrants.

'Pots and pots of lovely jam they were going to make,' she cried. 'Now look at them filling that beast's stomach to bursting!'

Joanne, who'd managed to stop laughing at Mrs Widdowson's phraseology, put her arm round its neck and tried to tug it away from the rows of bushes. Not a centimetre did it budge. Then she tried coaxing it with a carrot she persuaded Mrs Widdowson to sacrifice from her vegetable store: but, plainly, the donkey preferred the taste of fruit to vegetables. Loving entreaties whispered into those wagging ears had no noticeable effect, either. Stolidly, the donkey chewed on through every enticement.

'Look, it must have an owner, it must live near by to have got here, so why don't we find somebody who *knows* it and ask them to fetch it, to take it home?' Lee suggested with what seemed to him to be the brightest thinking of the night.

'Its owner is away and that's why I'm looking after it,' Mrs Widdowson admitted surprisingly. 'It lives in the field beyond the end of the garden. Must have followed me after I'd been feeding it and broken through my fence, the ungrateful beast!'

'Does he have a name?' Joanne wanted to know.

'Clarence. Silly name for a donkey in my opinion but, well, there you are, it *is* a silly donkey and –'

'Look, we can't stay here all night, Mrs Widdowson,' Lee cut in. He was becoming exasperated with their lack of success. Moreover, he was aware that it was getting late and his mother wouldn't be pleased if he wasn't home very soon. 'There's one trick that's bound to work – I was reading about it recently in a book about a lonely trek across the Sahara. If we light a fire under the donkey's belly that'll –'

'You'll do no such thing!' Mrs Widdowson shrieked. 'You'd be arrested for cruelty in no time

– and no doubt the police would say I'd been aiding and abetting. Out of the question.'

All three now stared helplessly at the donkey. Clarence, totally unaware of the dire fate being recommended for him, began to dismantle another bush.

'Oh, but there is another shock treatment we could try,' cried Joanne, suddenly inspired. 'Most animals hate noise, especially a loud, unexpected noise. May I borrow your dustbin lid, Mrs Widdowson?'

With evident lack of enthusiasm for such a notion, the cottage owner nodded. At speed Joanne

went to the bottom of the garden and there found, to her delight, two dustbins. Grabbing the lids, she stole up on Clarence's blind side and then, with melodramatic timing, clashed them together like cymbals.

The effect on the donkey was electrifying. One moment he was munching happily, the next he was galloping frenziedly down the path to his own field, braying in apparent terror. Delighted with her instantaneous success, Joanne followed, still banging away with the lids, to make sure he didn't halt before he was well clear of the garden.

'I think that's quite enough of that,' Mrs Widdowson called out to her. 'The wretched donkey's been removed so you can calm down, young lady. And go and put those lids back on the dustbins. I don't want my sleep disturbed tonight by cats raiding the bins.'

Lee raised his eyebrows and then shrugged his shoulders: Mrs Widdowson hadn't even had the decency to say thank you for the good work Joanne had accomplished. All she could do was find something else to complain about.

'Come on, Jo, let's get off home,' he said, softly but urgently. 'It's late enough already.'

Rather grudgingly, it seemed to Lee, Mrs Widdowson allowed them to pass through her cottage again to reach the alleyway. With exaggerated politeness, they both wished her good night and

131

no further trouble with Clarence. The front door slammed shut behind them and they distinctly heard the noise of a bolt being shot home.

A stride from the gate Lee came to an abrupt halt: so abrupt that Joanne cannoned into him. For a moment or two all he could do was stare with disbelief. He couldn't speak.

His motorcycle had vanished.

Two

'But it can't just have disappeared on its own like that,' Lee said for the umpteenth time in sixty seconds. He still found it impossible to believe the evidence of his eyes.

'Come on, Lee, start thinking intelligently,' Joanne told him as she widened the search area by peering into neighbouring gardens and under hedges. 'Somebody, some *person*, has moved the bike – maybe just for a joke or something. But – '

'Some joke!' Lee exploded. 'That bike's the most precious thing in my life. Anybody who touched it without my permission would be a *criminal*. There's nothing in the world *funny* about having a bike pinched – and it must have been pinched, Jo. Some rotten swine has ridden off on it!'

Joanne frowned. 'I think we'd have heard if somebody started the engine and rode away. I mean, it is fairly loud and – '

'In the din you were making with those lids we

133

couldn't possibly have heard anything else,' Lee pointed out sharply. 'Anyway, they could have just wheeled it down the road for a bit and then started it up there.'

There was nothing to be gained by arguing, Joanne realised. She really had supposed that the culprit was simply having a bit of fun at their expense. Now she was inclined to agree with Lee that the bike had been stolen. Unhappily, when they'd discovered the loss there had been no one in sight who might have been able to explain what had happened. Moreover, the entire place still seemed to be deserted.

'Look, I think we'd better go and report this to the police without further delay,' Joanne suggested. 'They might be able to put out a radio call or something to their patrol cars to be on the look out for the bike. They might even *know* somebody who makes a habit of stealing motorcycles and go and catch him before he can flog it or change its appearance or something. Speed off the mark is always said to be absolutely vital in solving a crime. O.K.?'

'I suppose so,' he responded glumly. 'But maybe we should use Mrs Widdowson's phone and dial 999. That'd be quicker.'

'Oh no! In the first place, the 999 system is for real emergencies, matters of life-and-death. We'd be in worse trouble if we tried that. And in the second

134

place, I very much doubt if the old Widdowson would answer the door to us. Now she's got what she wants she won't want to know us, I'll bet. So, come on, let's get down to the police station.'

The light was on over the front door but it was some time before anyone answered their ring. 'I hope this is a proper inquiry because I was just about to go off duty and I don't like to be disturbed for nothing,' said the man Lee recognised as Sergeant Wilde. 'And, anyway, shouldn't youngsters of your age be safely tucked up in bed by this time?'

'We're not as young as that, Sergeant!' Joanne protested. 'We are both at secondary school. Anyway, we've come to report the theft of a valuable motorcycle. It's just happened so the thief can't be far away yet. If you hurry you – '

'Hang on, hang on! Whose motorcycle are we talking about, to start with? The one who's suffered the loss is the one who should be reporting it.'

'It's mine, actually,' Lee admitted rather tentatively. 'But it's a scrambles bike, you know, for motocross. I'm a member of the Skalbrooke Schoolboy Motorcycle Club. I was just wheeling it home, pushing it past Mrs Widdowson's cottage when – '

'You're sure, lad, you weren't *riding* it home?' the policeman cut in. 'That would be an offence at your age and – '

'Sergeant, if my cousin here had been riding it

135

nobody could have stolen it, could they?' pointed out Joanne, doing some cutting in of her own. 'We both know what the rules are and we abide by them.'

Sergeant Wilde frowned and gave her an appraising stare. He must have approved of what he saw because he didn't pursue the matter of illegal riding. Instead, he asked Lee to describe in detail what had happened and then give a description of the bike. Much of it he wrote down, including the code number that Uncle Ken had marked both under the saddle and under the petrol tank. Momentarily, Lee had been doubtful about disclosing that number but he supposed it would be safe enough with the police.

'Well, I don't rate your chances very high of getting it back,' the sergeant announced eventually. 'You'll be very lucky if you do, young man.'

Lee was staggered by that remark. 'But, surely, it can't be far away – and every policeman will recognise it from that description I've given you.'

This time Sergeant Wilde not only raised his eyebrows; he almost managed a smile. It would, however, have been a wry smile.

'Do you have any idea,' he asked, 'how many motorcycles are stolen in this country every year?'

'Er, no.'

'Well, then, be prepared for a surprise. Because the total is over fifty thousand. And that represents a figure of one motorcycle stolen just about every nine minutes, day or night. But, of course, most of them are taken at night, as yours appears to have been.'

This time, Lee was so astonished that he couldn't make any reply at all. He couldn't understand how the police officer could be so calm about things when motorcycles were being stolen on that scale.

'But most of them will be found, won't they?' Joanne asked hopefully, trying to find some way of comforting Lee.

Very slowly, very solemnly, Sergeant Wilde shook his head. 'Fewer than two thousand, I'm afraid. On average, only one bike recovered for every twenty-five nicked.'

'Yes, but that'll be in big cities, won't it?' Lee said. 'I mean, in a small place like this, well, somebody's bound to spot it sooner or later, aren't they?'

'I hope so for your sake, son. But, you see, most of the thieves act pretty smartly to conceal the evidence. Either the bike's given a new overcoat of paint to disguise it or it's dismantled – cannibalised, in many cases, to provide spare parts for other bikes, making them as good as new. Oh yes, that's quite a racket. So don't put your hopes up too high. Like I said, the odds are stacked agin yer.'

'But you'll do your best, won't you?' Joanne asked anxiously.

'Oh, we *always* do that, young miss, whatever some folk think,' said Sergeant Wilde, smiling at last. 'Yes, of course we'll do all we can to get that green-and-silver monster back on the road – er, the scramble circuit.'

'Thanks very much,' said Lee gloomily. At that moment, he thought he might have seen the last of his beloved bike. It was terrible to imagine some villain taking it to pieces and disposing of the best bits for the highest prices.

'Oh, by the way, we'll let you know if there's any news,' Sergeant Wilde called as Joanne was about to close the front door behind them. 'There's
138

no need for you to call here every day to ask what's happening.'

'In other words, don't come bothering us about a mere scrambles bike when we've more important crimes to investigate,' Lee muttered sarcastically.

In spite of Joanne's reminders that his mother would be increasingly concerned about the lateness of their return, Lee couldn't be hurried on the rest of the way home. He paused constantly, simply to listen, almost praying that he'd hear a recognisable engine note; though he realised that even if he did he was hardly in a position to chase after the bike and catch it up. He tried to believe there was still a chance that *somebody* had hidden it for a joke and that, somewhere along the route, he'd find it again.

Although Mrs Parnaby certainly mentioned the time in a disapproving way she didn't go on about it unduly. She had some news of her own: there'd been a phone call from her husband on the other side of the world.

'All being well, he'll be home next month,' she told them happily. 'He's picking up a new ship, a refrigerator ship, in New Zealand. It was a lovely clear line for once, almost sounded as if he was next door. And he was hoping to have a word with you, Lee. He spent ages talking to Darren instead.'

Lee was wise enough now to keep his thoughts

on that subject to himself. Even if he had been at home when the call came, his father would still have talked longer to Darren.

Dutifully he asked a few questions about his father's recent exploits at sea and then, without giving too much emphasis to the matter, explained that they'd been to the police station to report the probable theft of Lee's bike. Mrs Parnaby was sym-pathetic but of the opinion that it would turn up soon enough. She wasn't wildly enthusiastic about her sons' devotion to scrambling but she tolerated it; with her husband being away from home so much she was grateful to Joanne's father for all that he did to enable the boys to enjoy the hobby, as she thought of it.

When, at last, Lee went up to the bedroom he shared with his brother, Darren was scanning a horror comic. But he quickly put it down in order to recount the details of the chat he'd had with his father; inevitably, he chortled over the fact that Lee had missed the phone call altogether. Eventually, after he'd exhausted that topic, Darren, the elder by one year and one day, asked whether anything interesting had happened that evening at the Skal-brooke circuit.

Lee, who'd just climbed into bed and switched off his own light, decided he might as well disclose the news of the tragedy now. Darren would have to know sooner or later. So he provided a very brief, edited version of the events since Mr Shearsmith had dropped him off in the village.

He could guess Daz's reaction: and Daz didn't let him down. He jerked upright, eyes wide, expressing first amazement, then scorn. It hadn't taken him long to work out that Lee's loss could be his own gain; with his brother out of the way, Darren would stand a better chance of winning a motocross.

'Well,' he concluded, sounding almost triumphant, 'you're good at losing races, Lee – and now you're just as good at losing a bike!'

'I've won more races than you! And that's what counts,' Lee retaliated. Then he turned over heavily to indicate that the conversation was at an end.

Darren, however, always tried to have the last word. With a fiendish grin he called: 'Well, you won't be winning any more if you haven't got a bike, will you? And who's going to buy you a replacement?'

Lee pulled the sheet up over his head. In the depth of his despair at that moment he could even believe that Darren himself had organised the theft of the beautiful green-and-silver motorcycle.

Three

As the car park began to fill up at the next meeting
of the Skalbrooke Schoolboy Motorcycle Club Lee
muttered some excuse to the friends who'd brought
him and wandered off on his own. He wanted to see
as many bikes as possible rolled out of the vans and
removed from the trailers. It was, he knew, absurd
to think that any of his fellow members of the club
could have stolen his machine and then brought it
to the track for their own use. Yet he couldn't stop
himself from glancing at every transporter bus and
trailer just in case a miracle had happened. Naturally, he did it as discreetly as possible. It would be
terrible if anyone realised what was in his mind.

For Lee, it had been the longest week of his life:
the longest and the darkest. He'd resisted every
impulse to visit the police station in the village and
inquire how the search was going. Of course, he
knew how it was going: because the police hadn't
contacted him. So, plainly, the bike had vanished
142

without trace. Perhaps, by now, it was in a hundred pieces, scattered the length of the country, with the vital components contributing to other people's scrambles. But he didn't really believe that. He had to believe that the bike, his bike, was still as he'd last seen it, albeit in someone else's possession.

Now, he headed for the paddock and wondered whether Joanne would turn up. Her parents had returned from their Paris trip the previous day and Uncle Ken had promised to bring Darren to the meeting as usual. No doubt he would have something to say to Lee about the loss of the machine he'd bought for him.

It was the sort of dry, sunny day that, following a week without rain, provided the fast track conditions that Lee liked best. It seemed to him now that even the weather was conspiring against him; had it been pouring down and turning the circuit into a glue-pot he might, just might, have felt a little better. A small crowd was gathering by the control van close to the starting area. Many of the riders, he knew, would be reserves, hoping, probably actually *praying*, for someone not to turn up so that they could compete in the absentee's place. Well, one of them at least was going to be lucky: he or she would be able to ride in the Intermediates' events instead of the brilliant, lightning-fast, stop-at-nothing, internationally famous rider Lee Parnaby. After thinking that up, Lee tried a sarcastic laugh;

but it was such a dreadful effort that he nearly choked himself.

Automatically, he paused beside the 'For Sale' tables on which was laid out a great quantity of merchandise of all kinds: sets of riders' leathers, helmets with new-style visors, boots, knee-pads, both new and second-hand, sets of tools for budding mechanics. It was from such a stall, he remembered, that Joanne had bought him a lucky mascot just before he won his first race at the club. He fingered it now in his pocket: a key-ring with a leather tab cut in the shape of a cat. Lee twisted the strip of leather fiercely and decided it hadn't brought him much luck lately. Perhaps he should get rid of it, throw it away when no one was looking; he didn't suppose Jo would actually ask him if he'd still got the key-ring.

'Fancy a new helmet, then, Lee?' a voice inquired cheerfully as he was turning away from the tables. 'The new material this one's made of is terrific. So light you'd hardly know you're wearing it. Go on, give it a try – once you've tried this kind you'll never want any other sort!'

'If I'm not riding a bike I don't need a helmet, do I?' retorted Lee, turning away sharply. 'And I can't ride a bike if I haven't *got* one.'

The tone was savage enough to cause the salesman to blink. In the past he'd sold Lee a number of items of equipment and come to regard him as a

144

pleasant, easy-going boy with a sense of humour. Plainly, Lee Parnaby wasn't his usual self today.

On a low-loader parked at the edge of the selling area stood a 100 c.c. Honda, its red paintwork glistening in the sunlight. Lee couldn't avoid gazing at it wistfully. It was exactly the sort of machine that could carry him to success again in the Intermediates' race. It, too, was for sale – it was actually a second-hand bike – and the thought flitted through his mind that perhaps the owner would consider a hire-purchase deal. He tried to calculate how much would be needed for each instalment. Was there a chance that Uncle Ken would agree to meet the cost?

A moment later Lee shook his head to clear it of such stupid ideas. Darren might have received a favourable response if he'd needed financial help because he was Uncle Ken's favourite nephew – always had been and, presumably, always would be. Originally, Uncle Ken had thought that Darren was the superior rider if only because he was the elder; then, when Lee had proved otherwise by his victories on the track, Uncle Ken had stuck to his first choice because Daz needed support and encouragement as the underdog! That, anyway, was how Joanne had summed up the situation – and she knew her own father pretty well. No, Lee concluded, there was little point in asking his uncle to help him to acquire a new motorcycle. His only hope of riding again was to find the one that had been stolen.

He tried to chat with a few of his pals and rivals but they were really too busy to talk to him: tinkering with the engines of their own bikes or assisting their mechanics (invariably father or brother) to change a tyre or adjust the tension on a chain. Brake and clutch cables were being examined, nuts tightened, plugs given final attention; there was no time for idle gossip. Lee collected a few handfuls of sympathy from those who'd heard of his loss; but he didn't want them. All he wanted was some action. So he slouched away from the paddock, and all the frantic activity of those who were actually going *to race*, and made his way across the track to a vantage point where he could watch the Juniors hurtling towards their own ambitions.

Suddenly, there was a serious spill on the sharp left-handed bend right in front of him. A boy Lee recognised as Andy Appleton had been riding headlong into the corner in his usual fashion; then, at the last split-second, he had a change of heart, tried to brake as he turned the front wheel – and the outcome was inevitable. As Andy went sprawling across the track another bike, hotly pursuing him, cannoned into Andy's slithering machine. The man standing next to Lee leapt over the marker tape and on to the track to sort things out. The woman who'd been standing beside him, holding the flags in her

146

role as a marshal, seemed about to follow when he told her to stay where she was. Lee, however, thought some help was needed to sort out the tangle and prevent a worse pile-up for already there was hardly any room on the track for the following riders to squeeze through and continue in the race.

'Come on, son, come on, you're all right,' the man was assuring Andy as he lifted him bodily from the track. 'You've only got a shaking – be right as rain in no time.'

It was Lee who hauled young Appleton's bike from the centre of the track and then wheeled it to safety. In Lee's opinion Andy had been far too rash in his approach to the bend; on the other hand, the boy who liked to be known as 'Double-A' never lacked spirit and was always willing to have a go at any obstacle. Just as Lee cleared the track two of the slower riders collided right in front of him and so again he went to sort out the problem. Quite by chance, he'd chosen to spectate at the most incident-packed place on the entire circuit.

The St John Ambulanceman who'd been attending to some of the fallen riders was furious with the woman marshal. It was her husband who'd gone on to the track to rescue Andy and, according to the St John man, she'd been so interested in what was going on that she'd forgotten to put up the yellow flag to warn everyone that there was an accident. As a result of her negligence there'd very nearly been a worse pile-up.

'Oh, but I *did* wave my flag! Everybody must have seen it,' the woman protested, looking round for someone who might confirm her story. Her glance fell on Lee. 'You saw what action I took, didn't you? Lee Parnaby, isn't it?'

'Er, I didn't see anything,' Lee, taken by surprise, told her. He didn't want to get involved in a row. 'I was too busy. Sorry.'

He backed away in case she persisted – and bumped hard into somebody.

'Hey, look where you're going, son!' a man called in alarm. 'One accident's quite enough already.'

'Sorry,' Lee muttered again. Then, when he turned round, he saw what the man meant.

Carrying his son, Danny, over his shoulder in fireman's lift style, was Barry Millard, one of the Skalbrooke club's most enthusiastic supporters (he was also rumoured to be one of its wealthiest because he had his own business as a builder as well as a fleet of lorries). Danny was of Lee's age and a long-time rival. At a previous meeting, however, he'd smashed up his ankle, which was in plaster. He wasn't going to miss any of the action if he could help it, however, and that was why Mr Millard was prepared to carry him from vantage point to vantage point.

148

'How's it going then, Danny?' Lee inquired, glad to escape the attentions of the woman marshal.

'Oh, getting better, I expect. Just wish they'd let me ride, that's all – I mean, Dad could set it in concrete and the ankle'd be fine!'

It was plainly a joke he'd made several times already but Lee dutifully laughed. He couldn't help sympathise with a scrambler who'd broken an ankle. It was almost as bad as having a bike stolen. Still, a cracked ankle would mend eventually but there was no guarantee the missing machine would ever be seen again.

'Thought you'd be in the pits, tuning up your bike for the Intermediates' race,' observed Danny. 'Nothing wrong with you, is there, Lee?'

While Mr Millard settled his son on a convenient mound of grass so that he could watch the racing in relative comfort, Lee sorrowfully related the story of his own tragedy. Mr Millard asked a few pertinent questions about the efforts of Lee and the police and everyone else to trace the stolen bike. Danny said nothing, though his attention didn't seem to wander while Lee was talking.

'Couldn't your Uncle Ken have found a substitute bike for you, Lee?' asked Mr Millard sympathetically. 'I've always thought he looks after you and your brother very well – goes to a lot of trouble to keep you racing.'

'Er, afraid not, Mr Millard.' Lee didn't want to

150

say anything that could be regarded as criticism of his uncle. 'Uncle Ken and Aunt Sue have been away in Paris for a few days and only just got back.'

'Got your gear with you? Your boots and stuff?' Danny inquired unexpectedly.

'Well, some of it – the essential bits. I mean, I was just keeping my fingers crossed that the bike might turn up and then – '

'If you like, you could ride my spare bike, the Kawasaki. Better for it to be on the move than standing around doing nothing,' Danny offered. He said it in such a casual tone that Lee could scarcely believe he meant it.

'*Honestly*, Danny? You'd let me have it, just like that?'

'Oh sure. You're a good rider so you won't bash it around. Like I said, it might as well be tuned up by racing than sitting in the van. It'll be O.K. if Lee takes it, won't it, Dad?'

Mr Millard nodded emphatically. 'Was just going to suggest the same thing myself. No point in your being immobilised, Lee, when we can help out. In any case, we brought the bike with us for, er, well, for an emergency, let's say. Look, now that you're settled and comfortable, Dan, I'll take Lee over to the car park so he can get the old Green Meany started. Won't be long.'

Before Lee could exhaust himself in uttering endless thanks for Danny's kindness, Barry Millard

151

steered him across the track and in the direction of the paddock and park.

'It's not in bad shape even if I say so myself,' grinned Mr Millard as he lifted the green-and-white Japanese machine out of the van. 'I reckon you could do a lot worse than ride this one, Lee. Anyway, it'll give us all a chance to see what it's capable of.'

Lee reached for it with the reverence he felt for the most powerful and desirable motorcycle in the world. Only a quarter-of-an-hour earlier he'd been thinking of himself as the unluckiest member of the Skalbrooke Schoolboy Motorcycle Club. Now, as a result of literally bumping into Danny Millard and his dad, he was surely the luckiest. Against all the odds, he was going to race again immediately.

'Look, you'd better get over to the control van and let the officials know about the change of bike and so on,' Mr Millard advised. 'Then, pick up your gear. If there's anything extra you need I expect you'll find it in the back of our van. We always keep a pile of spares. Danny-boy can be a bit tough on knee-pads and shoulder protectors! Right, Lee, off you go then. Oh, and just remember – we'll be cheering you on every time you come past us. You'll be giving Danny an extra, personal interest in the racing while he's laid up.'

Lee bounded away with all the exuberance of a spring lamb. He wished that Joanne would turn up so that he could share his joy with her. In fact, it was her father that he met, face to face, as he came away from the control van.

'Ah, Lee, I was looking for you,' Uncle Ken began, his face already creasing into a frown. 'We need to have a serious talk.'

'Sorry, Uncle, but do you think it can wait until after the first race?' Lee answered blithely. 'I need to get the bike warmed up, you see, and well, there isn't much time.'

'Oh, so you've *found* your bike then?' Mr Wragby said in a warmer voice. His face now brightened again. 'Well, that is – '

'Er, no, not exactly, Uncle,' Lee cut in warningly. 'But I'll explain everything later. Oh by the way, did you have a good time in Paris?'

'That all depends,' was the heavy reply. 'It depends on what happened here in my absence. Darren's been telling me all about your – '

'Yes, well he would, wouldn't he? But I'll tell you the *truth* when I've beaten Daz again in this next race.'

Four

Lee was feeling rather less confident about the outcome of the race as he sat astride the Kawasaki,
waiting for the elastic tape to zip sideways to signal
the start. He had a poor draw in the middle of the
line of riders. Because the first bend was an acute
left-hander he needed a flying start to pull ahead of
those bikes on his left. But, of course, he couldn't
be sure just how his new machine would respond
when he let it go. On a tight course such as this one
the early leaders had a considerable advantage so
long as they remained calm. Often Lee had heard
it argued that a race on this circuit was usually
decided on the first lap. So the first essential was to
make a lightning dash from the gate.

Graham Relton, whose supremacy in his age-
group Lee had challenged in recent events, was
immediately on his left. Behind his visor his eyebrows had visibly shot up on catching sight of the
machine Lee was riding. There'd been no opportunity for an exchange of comments but Lee had no
154

doubt at all that Graham would take comfort from the fact that his rival was mounted on an unfamiliar bike. Lee, for his part, had hoped to conceal the change until the race was well under way; then, if he could outwit Graham at some stage, it would be doubly satisfying, not least because Gray perhaps wouldn't recognise the new combination of rider and bike from the rear! Now, of course, that ambition was dashed.

The tension that was always present at these times was tightening its grip on him – and probably every other rider alongside him. He moistened his lips, tried to ease his fingers inside the gauntlets, adjusted the throttle yet again for the perfect take-off and prayed he'd be in luck.

Despite his almost desperate determination to lead the field into the first bend, Lee was actually one of the last to move. Somehow he hadn't seen the tape snap away and it was Graham's surging back wheel that alerted him to the fact that the race had started. Kerry Todd, the throttle-happy girl on his right, shot away ahead of everyone on her Yamaha.

Lee, feeling the rear-wheel spin but achieving no acceleration, bounced on the saddle – and this time the power was there. His heart, though, was sinking as he headed into the cascade of dust sent up by flying tyres. He had made a complete hash of things in his first race on the Green Meany.

Then, as visibility improved and he began to think about his racing line for that first bend, he realised that the bikes ahead of him were slowing and, in one or two cases, turning broadside on to him. In almost the same instant he spotted the red flag being waved vigorously to recall the field. Lee breathed again! There had been a false start. Someone had anticipated the starter's signal and that was why Lee hadn't seen the movement of the tape; and he wasn't alone in that.

Once again the nervous excitement built up swiftly as, with the line re-formed, the riders awaited their dash towards glory – or grief. Lee was worried that his bike wasn't going to provide him with anything like the performance he could expect from his own machine. He suspected there was plenty of power to be called on – Danny Millard wouldn't have tolerated anything less – but it might take time to find out how best to control it. And time was really not on his side.

This time he was alert enough to discern the slight movement of the starter's shoulder as he released the tape. There was no free spin of the back wheel – he was away and helping to create the great cloud of blue smoke from roaring exhausts that would hang above the starting gate for quite some time.

Into the first corner he went as one of the leading batch – hardly a wheel's width behind Graham

Relton. Kerry Todd, too, had got a flier. The Yamaha cut in on Lee as they shuddered powerfully through the angle and quickly built up speed again. Kerry was one of the newer riders in the club and Lee had a lot of respect for her tenacity and courage; she could, however, be dangerously headstrong at some bends where caution really was vital.

The Kawasaki came on strong as Lee risked going for a gap between the two riders directly ahead of him. If he didn't take his chance now it would probably vanish within seconds. He had learned not to hesitate when a genuine opening presented itself. Once again, the Green Meany responded with flowing acceleration and Lee had a trouble-free passage into sixth place.

The boy just in front of him was Robert Beaman, known to every other member of the club as Concorde, or Conky for short, simply because he spent so much time high in the air. Robert really loved a ribbed route because then he could fly all the time; it hardly appeared to concern him that, by spending so much time in the air, he was ruining his chances of success. He enjoyed going upwards and that was that. Lee knew that he could overtake Conky almost at will. So that was one rider ahead of him he didn't have to worry about.

The next real test was the hairpin where Danny Millard and his father were keeping watch.

157

Although he guessed that they'd give him a wave and a cheer Lee was going to take no risks by responding in any way at all. He'd treat the U-turn with caution and so demonstrate that he was handling Danny's bike with care. The time to throw it about would come when he was in contention for the lead on the final lap.

Although his rear wheel took a knock from a bike that was striving to overtake, Lee negotiated the turn without difficulty and moved up through the gears. He was finding the clutch a little strange but, he supposed, that was to be expected on a new machine. All the same, it seemed to him to be slipping at times. Probably it simply hadn't occurred to Mr Millard to warn him of the Green Meany's individual peculiarities.

The thrusting rider behind him was again making a determined effort to get past and, this time, Lee took a quick glance in an effort to identify him. Much to his surprise, it was Darren. Whether Darren recognised him he couldn't tell. Certainly he gave no sign that he knew who was directly in front of him – or, as Daz himself would undoubtedly put it, obstructing him. What surprised Lee was that his brother wasn't already in the leading group for he invariably got off to a flying start; it was later in a race that his troubles tended to occur. Perhaps on this occasion he'd been caught out by the false start and been unable to achieve a second successive fast

158

break. Now, of course, he would be determined to make up for missed opportunities to keep pace with Gray Relton.

Although he was just as keen as anyone else to win the motocross Lee couldn't resist the thought of keeping Daz at bay for as long as possible. It was a perfectly legitimate tactic to prevent a rival from overtaking you and Lee could just imagine Daz's fury if someone succeeded in holding him off for an entire circuit; it would be all the more pleasurable if Daz didn't know for sure who was responsible – until later, anyway.

Lee was certain he knew just where his brother would attempt to overtake. It would be on an uphill section out of a sharp right-hand corner across the camber. The climb was over exposed tree roots and led to a wooded section where the track naturally narrowed. A burst of power up that stretch should carry any front-runner clear of slower, or down-hearted, opponents. Lee intended to cut Daz off and then have the great joy of soaring away up the gradient – after letting his brother see just who had cut him off! Now that he was racing again, even though it wasn't on his own bike, he was experiencing a tremendous sense of sheer happiness. Apart from one or two minor qualms, he had no doubt now that the Kawasaki was a fine machine, well tuned and capable of putting any rider in the forefront of the field.

With controlled bursts of speed and fractional changes of his racing line, Lee kept just ahead of his brother's Yamaha. He could visualise every grimace and snarl in Daz's repertoire. Well, none of his ferocity was going to help him now because Lee wasn't going to yield so much as a centimetre to let him through.

By now, the leaders were out of sight. Lee supposed that among them would be Greg Shearsmith as well as Graham Relton, Kerry Todd and Concorde Beaman. Soon Conky would be in his element because at the approach to the right-hander there was a series of ripples on a slight downhill run. He would really fly those! With a bit of luck, Lee would follow suit.

Now the track swung away almost lazily to the left and back again and then Lee had the vicious right-hander in his sights. With Daz pushing strongly for an opening Lee opened up the throttle again to give himself the advantage of a slightly longer lead.

He was, he realised, going rather faster than he should to meet such a hazard; but, by this stage, he was quite confident he could cope with the situation. He felt he and the Kawasaki blended extremely well.

Instinctively he braked as the ground suddenly fell away from him. But, as he did so, his thumb rolled away and caught the throttle. With the front

wheel locking and the back thrusting ahead the outcome was inevitable.

Slewing violently, the Green Meany pitched Lee sideways. Astonishingly, he still managed to hold on to the machine and was in the act of pushing himself upright again when Darren cleverly swerved past him. In that same instant, Daz saw who it was – and without further thought put the boot in by kicking his brother out of the way. Later he would claim that he was simply steadying himself as he came close to toppling from his Yamaha because of the tricky manoeuvre he'd had to make.

But even as he crashed to the ground, Lee knew exactly what had happened. He couldn't really blame Daz for what he'd done. After all, he was the one who'd caused Daz's frustration and resultant anger.

Other riders, too, swept by as Lee got to his feet. To his great relief he found that he wasn't hurt in any way, apart from a slight ache in his shoulder. No doubt he'd wrenched a muscle as he tried to keep the bike upright. The engine was still running sweetly, the framework appeared to be unmarked, the rear wheel continued to spin.

'How are you, son?' asked an anxious voice as hands helped him to his feet. 'You were really going a bit crazy there, weren't you? Much too fast for safety.'

'It was a mistake,' Lee tried to explain hastily.

162

'It's not my bike and I must have touched the throttle when I was actually braking – easy to do if your hand slips. Look, I'm O.K., really. I want to get back into the race.'

No one, at that point, was trying to stop him. Once a rider was seen to be still in good shape and determined to keep riding he was encouraged by the marshals to do so. Luckily, the spill hadn't brought disaster to anyone else and so Lee had plenty of help from onlookers and the St John Ambulanceman as well to get back into the saddle and rejoin the pursuit of the pack. But now, of course, he was one of the tail-enders. His hope of finishing the scramble among the leaders – and ahead of Daz – was now of the slenderest kind.

The shoulder he'd half-landed on, and which he'd once injured before, protested slightly as he lifted the bike through the last of the ripples and then began to build up pace for the attack on the uphill section. This was one of the toughest parts of the track and the juddering effect of riding over the tree roots put a great strain on rider and machine. Lee had known several rivals come to grief at this point and even now a dazed looking boy in a blue helmet who'd parted company with his Suzuki was being attended to by the bushes.

To Lee's dismay, the bike's response when they started on the steep climb was weak. Moments before he'd been sure he had plenty of power and there was no suggestion that the engine was misfiring. Yet the bike seemed to have no zip at all. Even one of the complete duffers went past him with a triumphant air. Lee switched his line to avoid the keenest incline and that helped; so he began to weave instead of keeping an arrow-straight course. All the same, he knew he would never get back into the thick of the action if he had to keep making adjustments like that.

Moments earlier he'd been feeling thankful that Danny Millard and his father hadn't been in a position to witness his disaster at the right-hander; now he rather wished he could ask them whether the Green Meany was usually temperamental on severe uphill sections or was simply being ridden in the wrong manner. Lee was aware that some machines had special peculiarities, just like human beings, and until a rider was used to them he didn't really know what to expect in various situations. Perhaps the Kawasaki needed to be nursed a little before being asked for maximum thrust.

He continued through the wooded area at the top of the hill without further trouble. The track was firm, if rather bumpy in places, and gradually he was able to build up speed and even pass a few stragglers. By now he had no idea at all how the race was progressing but he supposed that Daz would be chasing the leaders hard even if he were not one of them himself. When he recollected

Darren's speed of reaction, and his excellent balance during the skirmish at the bottom of the incline he could only admire his brother's performance. He really hadn't imagined that Daz was capable of producing such skills under pressure.

Shortly he sped past the point where Uncle Ken had stationed himself in order to give Daz any information he could about what was happening during the race – and indicate if necessary when he should close up on those in front. Lee doubted that his uncle realised who was riding the Kawasaki at the moment it went past him. Just as well, Lee reflected; he didn't want to be noticed in a hopeless position.

He had just completed, in very smooth fashion, a fast switchback and was planning to turn on the juice when the race came to an abrupt halt – for Lee Parnaby. It came about quite unexpectedly. Sailing contentedly over the rise of the next fairly shallow incline he was startled to come upon two tangled bikes that were almost completely blocking the track. The riders were on their feet beside the horizontal machines and appeared to be arguing fiercely with one another while a marshal struggled to separate them. The boundary tape had been removed and, it seemed to Lee, the route switched to the right to avoid the squabbling motocrossers.

'Yes, that's the way now, go right, go *right*,' the marshal yelled at him after sensing his bewilderment. He pointed to the gap with his flag and Lee needed no further bidding. After all, like every other member of the club, he was used to obeying the instructions of officials who were conscious of safety requirements above all else.

Almost at once he sensed he'd taken the wrong course: that he'd misunderstood the official's signal. As he bounced over the thick, springy grass that formed a mound in the centre of the circuit he realised that no other bike had travelled that way – or, at least, not as part of the motocross. Too late he remembered from his previous explorations of the area on foot that, on the far side of the mound, were the remains of old quarry workings.

The land fell away at one point like the rim of a cliff.

Desperately, Lee braked hard. The back wheel slithered away from him on the grassy surface and this time Lee was unable to stay with the bike. He was flung sideways and into the tough, thick roots of a gorse bush. The engine cut instantly.

For several moments Lee simply lay where he had landed. Fortunately, his clothing protected him from the spiky gorse. He studied the bike that, he knew now, had let him down. The rear wheel was motionless and, for the first time, Lee really looked hard at the tyre – and saw that the nobbles were practically non-existent. No wonder there hadn't been much grip! That tyre ought to have been re-placed long ago.

Oddly enough, both the owner of the bike and the marshal who'd misdirected Lee arrived on the scene at the same moment, but from opposite direc-tions.

'You weren't supposed to come over here, this isn't part of the course,' the official said in an agi-tated manner to Lee. 'I was trying to channel you round that ridiculous pile-up. Couldn't you see that?'

'But the marker tape was missing,' Lee pointed out. 'I thought there was a good reason why the course had been changed.'

'Yes, that was a mistake,' the man now admitted.

Then, as if to defend his status, he added: 'But a boy of your experience – and intelligence – should have realised that. Everybody else went the proper way. Anyway, you're not hurt, are you?'

Lee shook his head. Satisfied that he'd done all that could be expected of him, the marshal departed sharply to take up his duties again.

'Not your day, is it, Lee, old son?' remarked Mr Millard with a grin. Once again he was supporting his son in a fireman's lift. The restless Danny had decided he wanted to move again to another viewing point. 'The old bike didn't let you down, though, did it?'

Lee wasn't quite sure how to answer. After all, they had been kind enough to lend him the machine in the first place. Mr Millard might be insulted if told that the rear tyre was in a terrible state and should never have been raced on.

'Er, no, it was pretty good really,' answered Lee, trying to sound enthusiastic about the Green Meany. 'Perhaps, though, I didn't quite get the hang of handling it. I mean, I think that's why I finished up here!'

With what he hoped was a convincing laugh he at last got to his feet. Once again his shoulder muscles protested mildly as he lifted the bike and examined it quickly for signs of damage. To his immense relief, it looked fine.

'I'll get it back to the car park for you, shall I?

Now that I'm out of this race there's not much point in going on riding it. I've no chance of picking up enough points to finish among the leaders at the end of the day.'

'O.K., son,' said Barry Millard cheerfully. 'Sorry it didn't work out better for you. But at least you got a bit of a ride.'

Then, for the first time since he'd arrived on the scene, Danny spoke.

'Didn't expect you to get much further than this, anyway, Lee,' he remarked in a matter-of-fact tone. 'Not with a rear tyre as worn out as that one. We knew it wanted changing but we didn't know just how bad it was.'

Lee just stared at him but inwardly he was groaning.

'*Now* you tell me! Well, thanks very much for nothing!' was what he wanted to say. Somehow, though, he managed to keep silent.

Five

The sun was laying an orange carpet across the glistening meadow beside the river as Lee ran along the tow-path. Yet, in spite of that rising sun, there was still a chill in the air and he was already wishing he'd chosen to wear his track-suit instead of T-shirt and very abbreviated shorts. Still, he'd soon arrive at the start of the trim trail on the edge of Sonnington Park and the exercises he'd be doing there would definitely warm him up.

The early morning run was part of his campaign to improve his stamina and strengthen his leg muscles. Even before riding in his first race he guessed, from magazine articles he'd read, that motocross was a tough and demanding sport. Now, from experience he knew it was, and therefore physical fitness was a vital factor in the effort to be a successful rider. Running not only helped to increase lung capacity but strengthened leg muscles – and the legs had to be strong when a rider was directing a powerful bike over energy-sapping scrambles circuits. Lee also underwent a series of exercises with weights on a multigym at a leisure centre but he found that he enjoyed the running part of his fitness programme more than anything. From time to time he paused to do deep breathing routines that also helped what he described to various amused or interested onlookers as 'the oxygen intake situation – you see, how much oxygen you can absorb in a second or so is the real key to success in sport'. He'd yet to come across anyone who tried to deny that.

Of course, the odd self-proclaimed genius such as Darren scoffed at the notion that physical fitness was so important. According to Daz, the top motocross rider needed only skill on the bike and determination to stay at the top. Naturally, he included himself in that category and, at present, he had a point. He had finished runner-up to Graham Relton at the last club meeting when Lee hadn't even finished the course on his borrowed bike. To his own immense and noisy satisfaction, Daz had actually won one of the day's four races, though Gray had been unlucky that time with a broken chain. Inevitably, his brother was still making silly jokes about how 'little Lee has lost his machine and doesn't know where to find it!' It was no longer worth pointing out the stupid repetition within that sentence: if you'd lost something it naturally followed that you didn't know where it was.

As he left the tow-path and ducked under a rail fence bordering the Park he was reflecting that Darren had everything going for him at the moment: as a result of that first victory, he'd been promised a weekend trip with Uncle Ken that included a visit to some Rugby 'sevens' and a sea fishing expedition. Daz's immediate reaction was to announce that he'd return with a record catch. Although Uncle Ken hadn't been too severe about the loss of the bike – apparently it was insured, which was a consolation for him if not for Lee – he'd not extended the invitation to his younger nephew. Lee's time, he'd suggested, might be better spent 'making a proper search for that missing machine of yours'. Lee just nodded obligingly. In any case, he didn't care for team games and he much preferred his fish, complete with chips and vinegar, straight from a shop.

The trim trail was a new venture and although Lee didn't make a great deal of use of it he rather enjoyed watching some of the overweight, flabby adults try to sweat away a few pounds or get some response from almost non-existent muscles. There were three levels of attainment for the various tests, conveniently marked with red, yellow or green spots; but, because he wasn't trying to prove anything, either privately or in public, Lee simply chose those which would aid his own cause – such as the series of logs to be jumped in two-footed fashion, the step-up-and-step-down stile and then, just for fun, the parallel bars set at different heights. That was an exercise that really brought tears to the eyes of some of the joggers, who furtively had a go at one or two of the stiffest obstacles.

Lee exchanged friendly greetings with a couple of young-ish housewives who made a habit of having a morning run just for the pleasure of the outing – both were slim enough not to have to shed excess weight – and then settled down to his routine. Within moments he was glowing with his exertions. Carefully he felt his thigh and calf muscles after each test. He wrinkled his nose. His legs seemed as thin as ever. No extra muscle had developed as far as he could tell. Still, he *felt* quite strong – and the existing muscles didn't ache nowadays even after a long ride – so all must be well. And somebody had once said that *wiry* people were usually the toughest.

With his ankles hooked under a bar on a wooden frame he was carefully counting his way through a set number of sit-ups when a familiar voice interrupted his concentration.

'Hey, that's a terrific sight! Every Skalbrooke scrambler ought to see it. Otherwise, they'd never believe it!'

Lee hastily unhooked himself from the bar and got to his feet. He looked at his cousin in astonishınent; and then, realising how little he was wearing, in some embarrassment.

'Jo! What are you doing here? I mean, how on earth did you know where I was?'

'Oh, how *clever* of you to realise that I could only be here because I was looking for *you*,' Joanne replied with mock admiration. 'I'd clap my hands if I wasn't holding my sides to stop myself shaking to bits with laughter!'

'Come on, Jo,' said Lee, now beginning to get exasperated. 'Something's happened, hasn't it? You're in a – a funny mood. What is it?'

'Lee, I've got some news for you – and I think it may be good news,' she told him in a more restrained manner, though she still smiled. 'That's why I came pedalling down here like mad, to tell you as soon as possible. I knew you came here for a run so I thought I'd check before trying your home. Listen, don't build your hopes too high but it could be that your motorcycle's been found – well, spotted, anyway.'

'What! But where? Who's got it? Can we go and get it back now? Jo, this is terrific and –'

'Lee! I told you – don't get carried away. We could be wrong, very easily. It's got to be checked first, and that's not easy.'

'Oh, come *on* Joanne! There's no need to build up the suspense. This could be the best news I've had for – for years.'

174

'I'm just trying to be calm and careful, Lee, that's all. It's for your own good. Now just listen without interrupting and I'll tell you what I know. I was talking about you and your bike – just casually, nothing significant, so don't get any odd ideas about my talking about you all the time – now *don't* interrupt, Lee! As I say, I was mentioning it to Carolyn and she said that was interesting because her brother had been talking about a neighbour of theirs who's been riding around the farm on a new bike lately. Carolyn's parents are farmers, the other side of Lingdale, and this neighbour, a boy called Mike Collier, is supposed to be a bit of a wild guy at times. He's quite a bit older than us, seventeen or so, the same as Carolyn's brother, but he looks younger and he's not very big. That's important because the bike's fairly small, according to Carolyn. This Mike is actually using it to round up the sheep and lambs and that sort of thing!'

'What! But that's – well – a crime!'

Joanne grinned. 'It certainly is if it's *your* bike, Lee. Anyway, as I was saying, it's because Mike is using it a lot on the farm that Carolyn's family have seen it quite often. Well, when she told me that I asked her to check on it for me as much as she could – you know, see what colour it is, what make and whether Mad Mike Collier would reveal how he got hold of it. So she did and she rang me last night and the signs are good. Green-and-silver without a

175

doubt, your make and 100 c.c. But Mike himself is saying nothing about how he got hold of the bike, where he bought it or anything of that sort. In other words, he's being deliberately mysterious about its origin. Not much doubt, is there, that he's got something to hide. And that, Cousin Lee, is as much as I know at this moment. But not bad detective work, is it?'

'It's terrific, Joanne, absolutely terrific! I can hardly believe it's true, that's all. I mean, I'd never given up hope that it would be found but I must admit that after all this time without any news of any sort I was beginning to think I was wrong to keep hoping. Just shows, you should never despair. Mum always says that when she hasn't had a phone call from Dad for a long time. By the way, have you told anybody else about this yet?'

'Of course not!' she replied indignantly. 'It's your bike so you should be the first to know. You're the one who's been going through all the agony since it was swiped that night. I'd have phoned you last night but it was late when I got the news and my parents would have been suspicious if I'd telephoned anyone as late as that – Dad might even have casually-on-purpose eavesdropped! So, no, I didn't tell Dad.'

'Good. Knew you'd realise what I meant. Well, that means we can go and get it back on our own without anyone else telling us not to or causing
176

trouble. This guy sneaked it away from us when we weren't looking so we'll do the same thing to him. Seems dead fair, that. Real justice. Now –'

'Hang on a tick! I think you're forgetting something rather vital, Lee.'

He frowned. 'What's that?'

'Well, we don't *know* yet that it's your bike. We can only *assume* that from the evidence and the general, er, circumstances. Before we do anything rash – anything that might be criminal – we've just got to check it out, make absolutely sure it *is* yours.'

Thinking hard, Lee sat down on the sit-ups bench and stretched his legs out in front of him across the path. After a moment's hesitation, Joanne propped her bicycle against a tree on the other side of the path and then squatted down beside him. She hadn't wanted to say so, but she was very pleased that he apparently wanted to include her in his plan to recover the motorcycle.

Methodically, he asked for any other details she might have about Collier and the farm but all she could tell him was that it was called Top-of-the-Moors Farm and located quite close to the Army's practice range, something Carolyn mentioned from time to time. So far as Carolyn knew there was no regular pattern to Mike's riding of the bike; he simply used it when it was helpful in his farm work. She was fairly certain, though, that he didn't ride it away from the farm.

'Well, we've got to go and see it as soon as possible,' Lee announced in a very positive manner. 'So that means this evening, straight after tea. Somehow we'll have to get a close look at it even if this guy Collier isn't using it. You can get away, can't you, Jo?'

'Oh yes – yes, definitely,' she answered at once, trying not to think of the science test that would have to be written up for that evening's homework. 'We can get as near to the farm as possible on our bikes and then, well, make our way on foot. But we don't want to be seen if we can help it. Then no one will guess what we're up to.'

'Good thinking!' Lee said enthusiastically. 'We'll wear some camouflage. Oh, and binoculars could be very useful. Have you got any?'

She nodded. 'Dad has. He takes them on his fishing trips and watches sea birds. Well, that's what he claims. I've got other ideas. Anyway, I should be able to get hold of them for tonight.'

Lee jumped to his feet. 'Great! Right then, let's meet by the church at half-past six. Honestly, I don't know how I'm going to survive the agony of waiting until then!'

'Oh, I imagine the thought of seeing your magical motorbike again will keep you alive somehow,' grinned Joanne as she swung herself into the saddle of her cycle.

Six

The sense of excitement mingling with anxiety that
Lee had been trying to suppress all day finally bub-
bled over as he finished tea. In his haste to leave the
table he stumbled against a chair leg, put out a hand
to save himself and knocked the butter-dish to the
floor. Fortunately it didn't break and the butter
picked up only a small amount of fluff from the
carpet.

'What on earth's wrong with you today, Lee?' his
mother asked as she watched his desperate efforts
to remove evidence of the incident from both butter
and carpet. 'You've been like a cat on hot bricks all
through the meal.'

'Got to go out. Meeting Joanne at half-six, so I
don't want to be late.'

'Oh. Oh, well that's good. Going anywhere, er,
special?'

'Not really, Mum. Just want some fresh air, so
we're going for a bit of a spin on our bikes up
towards the moors.'

'Er, well that sounds a good idea, Lee. Give Joanne my love. But don't be back late. Remember you had a very early start this morning. Can't burn the candle at both ends, you know.'

As he had known it would, the reference to the outing with Joanne disarmed his mother. She thoroughly approved of the interest Lee showed in his cousin and the time he spent with her, especially as Darren could hardly be bothered to say a word to her even when she was a visitor in their home. But then, Darren was almost two years older than Joanne. Mrs Parnaby believed Lee's friendship with Jo was some recompense for the generosity her brother-in-law, Ken Wragby, was forever displaying towards her two motorcycle-mad sons.

Lee wasn't surprised that Joanne had arrived at the rendezvous ahead of him; she'd proved several times that she was an excellent time-keeper. She was wearing a heather-coloured sweater and had put her hair up under a bobble hat. From her saddle-bag she triumphantly produced a pair of binoculars.

'Great! But look at this,' Lee told her with equal pride. From under his light pullover he unwound an authentic camouflage jacket in two-tone mud-and-olive. 'Got it from a mate of mine, who borrowed it from his brother who was in the Army for a couple of years. Cost me a fair bit in cash and promises of free rides on the bike when I get it back

180

but I reckon it's worth it. If anybody notices us they'll think I'm a soldier off-duty and you're my girl friend for the night.'

'Gee thanks, I never thought you'd ask!'

'Come on,' he said quickly, worried that she might take the idea seriously. 'Let's get moving. The sooner we get there the more likely we are to see something.'

They pedalled briskly down the main street of the village, and though it crossed both their minds as they passed Mrs Widdowson's cottage that but for her trouble with the donkey they wouldn't have needed to set out on such a journey, neither of them mentioned it.

After a couple of miles they turned off the highway on to a narrow, deeply rutted dirt track that was obviously chiefly used by farm vehicles. Lee remarked jocularly that it would have served as a motocross course – if they'd been looking for one. After that they had to concentrate on conserving their breath for a hard climb out of a crater and Lee wished he could call on the power of his favourite engine instead of his legs. Beyond the rim of the crater they came across the first warning signs about the dangers of encroaching on the Army firing range which was spread over a large area of the moorland. Sometimes it was used for target practice by armoured vehicles, and the public was ordered to stay well clear of the boundary posts whenever red flags were flying to indicate that shooting was taking place.

Eventually the ground began to drop away and form into hollows and shallow-sided valleys. The bleakness of the upper slopes gave way to attractive grazing land and fields, bordered in some cases by dry-stone walls.

'That's where Carolyn lives,' said Joanne, pointing to a neat collection of buildings beside a tumbling stream. 'So the Colliers' place must be just over that brow.'

'Thank God for that,' replied Lee, glad of a pause even if it lasted only a second or two. 'I don't know how I found the energy to get as far as this!'

A couple of minutes later, however, his tiredness vanished as he gazed down on the farm where he believed his beloved motorcycle was hidden; because, distantly, he could hear an engine note he was positive he recognised.

On such a still evening sounds travelled a long way in the clear air and so it was some moments before the motorcycle came into view through a gap in the hedge surrounding one of the lower fields. By now Lee and his cousin were lying flat in a shallow depression. Lee trained the binoculars on the scene below but he hardly needed a second glance to know that the bike was his. Apart from the fact that the number plates bearing his personal number in white on a blue

background had been removed it was just as he'd last seen it.

He wanted to leap to his feet and cheer with his joy at seeing it again; but somehow he managed to restrict his delight to squeezing Joanne's arm and nodding furiously. She, of course, was just as happy as he was but something about the way the bike was being ridden puzzled her.

'Why is he going so slowly?' she whispered. 'Is he carrying something on the tank?'

Lee, who'd been too busy scrutinising the machine itself to take much notice of the rider, studied the scene again.

'It's a lamb!' he exclaimed a second later. 'It's a black one, too. He seems to be, well, almost cuddling it.'

She laughed. 'Well, it would be black, wouldn't it? I mean, anybody who could pinch your bike and just swan around on it like that is obviously the black sheep of his family! Oh yes, and they're called Collier, too, aren't they!'

After that it was difficult for her to suppress her fit of giggles. Although appreciating the joke Lee was far too intent on watching the rider's progress to add any comments of his own.

Much to his surprise, the bike was taken straight into a large barn on the far side of the yard. When, a few moments later, the rider emerged he was still carrying the lamb very carefully. He headed for the low, stone-built farmhouse and this time he didn't re-appear.

Although they kept watch for another quarter-of-an-hour, until the light began to fade as quite heavy clouds rolled up from the west, no one else was seen around the buildings. At one point, however, a typical black-and-white sheepdog limped across the yard as if taking a last sniff around before retiring for the night.

'If that was Mike Collier he acted in a very gentle way with that lamb,' Joanne remarked in a surprised tone. 'Not at all as I expected from Carolyn's description of him as a wild character. Can't be all bad, after all. I expect he's acting as the shepherd. That poor old sheepdog looks as though it's been hurt recently – or maybe it's just getting to the geriatric stage of life.'

Lee wasn't interested in such sentimental reflections. He had more pressing matters on his mind.

'Look, we could just sneak down there as soon as it gets really dark, grab the bike and ride off,' he suggested. 'I mean, if we just tell the police where the bike is *they* will come and collect it. But they'll hold on to it as evidence until the case comes up in court. So I won't be able to ride it for ages. You see, I asked a guy at school, whose father is a lawyer, what happened when the police recovered stolen property. He gave me all the details. That's why we've got to act for ourselves, Jo, and not get the police involved.'

She nodded. 'I know. I made some inquiries as well, Lee, just in case we were lucky enough to find your bike. It might even be difficult to prove that it really *is* your bike, even though *you* know that it is. The engine number may have been removed. But we can't just go and collect it tonight – no, hang on, Lee, let me finish. And remember, we've got to keep our voices down. Sounds carry in the open like this.'

Joanne paused, marshalling her thoughts. 'There are several reasons. One, it will soon be really dark and we can't risk riding it back to Lingdale over the moors in pitch-black conditions. Two, we can't just abandon our push bikes or manage to ride three bikes between us. Three, we know Mike Collier is up and about and probably the rest of his family are, too. They'd react fast if they heard the bike's engine and give chase. Remember, they wouldn't know we were just reclaiming your property. They'd suspect we were burglars! So there'd be a lot of fuss and we might not even get home tonight. And one last thing: I'm not used to getting up early in the morning like you and I must admit I'm now feeling pretty exhausted. I need my sleep tonight, Lee!'

He was on the point of yawning himself but he quickly covered that up by running his fingers through his thick helmet of honey-coloured hair and then scratching his scalp. Moreover, he'd been aware that his plan of action contained a few flaws.

'So what do *you* reckon we should do? And don't forget I want that bike to myself as soon as possible. I need to gets lots of practice in if I'm going to be chosen for the Inter-Club Championship. You know that's my great ambition.'

'Yes, I know all about that, Lee, and I'm taking it into account. Well, my idea is that we should make a dawn raid – no, not tomorrow but maybe the day after. Then we can really take them by surprise. We were learning in history about how armies attacked at first light and took the enemy completely by surprise. I know people on farms get up early but we can beat them to it with good planning. Also, I'm going to ask Carolyn to help by getting us some inside information about the layout of the farm and things like that. She may have been in that barn and know where a bike is kept – oh, and whether the door is locked. So what do you think of that?'

It appealed to him, especially the concept of making an early start. In any case, his brain was getting too tired to try and improve on the plan.

'It's great,' he told her with all the enthusiasm he could muster. 'We'll work out the details tomorrow. So, come on, let's get off home.'

By the time they reached the village they were

almost too weary to say good night to one another. Even so, Lee didn't find it easy afterwards to drop off to sleep. He couldn't stop thinking about the happiness he would experience when reunited with his bike.

It never occurred to him that something might go drastically wrong with their plans.

Seven

'I guessed Carolyn would be looking out for us this morning,' Joanne said with evident satisfaction as, two days later, she and Lee arrived at the farm. 'Look, she's up there at that first floor window, the end one on the right.'

Lee glanced up and could make out a dark-haired girl, apparently wearing a dressing-gown and with her arms tightly folded as if to ward off the cold. After briefly returning their wave she mimed the posture of sleep and then jerked a thumb over her shoulder.

'Must be her sister who shares her room,' Joanne explained. 'Otherwise I expect Carolyn would have been down to make a cup of tea for us. Pity she can't. I mean, dawn raiders are always supposed to go into action on a hot drink, aren't they? Or is it brandy!'

'I don't suppose,' said Lee heavily, 'that you'll be making jokes when we really start the action at Collier's place.'

'I only do it to help keep my courage up,' admitted Jo as lightly as she could manage. 'Anyway, better get the bikes into the tack room over there and then get on our way. It's getting lighter by the minute. I'd never have guessed the sun really got up as early as this.'

It was Carolyn who'd suggested that they leave their cycles at her farm when they carried out the mission that Joanne insisted on describing as the dawn raid. She'd promised that the cycles would be safe until they were able to retrieve them either that evening or at the weekend. That had neatly solved their problem of how to get to Top-of-the-Moors Farm at daybreak, though there'd still been the worry of waking early enough to set off in the dark. Fortunately, they'd both been able to get hold of alarm clocks (in Lee's case he swore he hadn't slept all night, anyway).

By dint of shrewd yet casual questioning of friends and contacts the ever-helpful Carolyn had discovered that Mike Collier was claiming, when asked, that he'd picked up the motorcycle by chance one evening when attending a party given by a group of young farmers at The Dog and Partridge Inn at Lingdale. His tale was that he thought it had been abandoned and as no one had come forward to claim it he now regarded it as his property. Naturally, Lee was furious when he heard that and Jo had some difficulty in calming him down. But it just proved, he said, what a cunning swine Mike Collier was and how he might have outwitted the police if they'd tried to reclaim the machine.

As they now left one farmyard and headed for another Joanne felt her nerves begin to jangle again. Her fingers tightened on the straps of the haversack she was carrying on her back: it contained some basic tools and a plastic bottle of fuel in case the bike ran out at a critical point in the escape. It had been agreed that they'd both ride but, of course, Lee couldn't have the haversack because then it would come between them. She kept glancing at the sky, watching the streaks of light widening as the day woke up.

They were wearing their camouflage gear again and although Joanne had put on a second sweater she still felt chilled; but that, she supposed, might be caused by apprehension. So far everything had gone almost too well; they hadn't met a single snag. Lee's confidence had waned a little in the interval since the first visit to the area of the farm but now it was advancing with the morning. From time to time he almost trembled with the joyous anticipation of riding his motorcycle once more.

Cautiously they came over the brow. There was no sign of life below; so, after an exchange of glances, they began the descent. They kept as close as possible to a meandering stone wall, in the hope that it might help to mask their approach should anyone glance out of one of the farm windows at the front. But, as far as they could tell, all the curtains were still drawn.

When they reached the corner of the yard Lee whispered 'Good luck, then, Jo'; and his cousin went ahead on her own. It had been agreed that she should check first whether the sheepdog, Luke, was in the barn. If so, she had a biscuit to give him as well as a friendly pat and a quiet word. Once again it was Carolyn who'd supplied the details about the dog; apparently it had a mild manner and would react favourably even to a stranger if offered a sweet biscuit. Luke was rather infirm now but had his own warm corner of the barn, which was never locked at night. Such lack of security seemed unwise to a town dweller but Joanne was thankful for it on this occasion.

Softly she called to the dog as she pushed open the door, and then winced as it gave a slight creak. Next moment a warm muzzle was thrusting into her hand for the biscuit.

'Well done, Luke, well done,' she told him, ruffling his coat. 'Yes, you really are an old softie, aren't you? But I'm really glad you are!'

He limped after her, back into the barn. Joanne had brought a torch and she needed it to help locate the motorcycle; it was in a stall at the far end of the building and covered by a horse blanket. She wasted no time examining it; that was Lee's job.

'Still all clear,' he told her as they changed places in the yard. 'I suppose if you're just looking after sheep you don't have to get up so early.'

That had occurred to Joanne but she hadn't wanted to raise false hopes by mentioning it earlier. Lee, taking the torch from her, went into the barn to check the bike and then move it into the open while she remained on watch. It had been decided that Lee shouldn't start the bike up in the barn unless a real emergency arose. If it could be wheeled out of earshot of the farm before they attempted to ride it then so much the better.

'It'd be marvellous, wouldn't it, if Collier went into the barn to get the bike and discovered somebody had *stolen* it in the night!' Lee had exulted when the raid was planned. 'That'd be real biter-bit justice.'

To his great relief, the bike appeared to be in perfect condition. If anything, it was cleaner than when he'd last ridden it. He couldn't hold back a surge of emotion now that he was touching it again. He ran his hand lovingly over saddle and tank and frame. Then, mindful of how vital every minute might be, he eased it out of the stall and wheeled it across the barn. He could tell that the tank was at least half-full of what a lot of the scramblers called 'go-juice' and so it seemed the supply they'd brought wouldn't be needed.

As he reached the doorway he paused to look in all directions, fearful that Jo might not have spotted that someone was keeping watch on the barn. Even though he was merely removing his own property it was difficult not to feel that he was acting like a criminal. All appeared clear, however, and Jo, looking gleeful, came across to close the huge door behind him. Luke watched, wagging his tail.

Lee's fear now was that the dog would start barking the moment they were clear of the farm buildings; or – and that might even be worse – chase after the moving bike as if trying to round it up like a wayward ewe. Jo, however, had anticipated that possibility and was keeping a supply of biscuits with which to quieten Luke at the critical moment.

Walking on either side of the bike they very slowly made their way down a sunken lane that ran beside the stream to the side of the farmhouse. In rather less than a hundred metres they should be out of sight of anyone looking out from any of the buildings. Luke had halted at the point where the lane inclined sharply downwards: he watched, still gently swishing his tail, with an air of some sadness. Jo was still praying that he wouldn't suddenly break into a furious round of barking. She wasn't sure what to expect of sheepdogs.

'Just keep your fingers crossed – everything crossed – that the engine fires first time and we can get a fast start,' Lee said to her in a whisper, as if they still might be overheard.

'Fast from the gate – you're good at that, Lee,' she encouraged him. 'Don't worry, I'm sure we'll make it now as long as we don't take silly chances.'

Walking the bike and keeping upright on such stony, difficult terrain was tiring work. Lee shifted his grip several times and kept looking back to see just how far they'd come. They'd agreed on a certain minimum distance they should travel before starting the engine; that had been an essential part of the plan and Lee knew he shouldn't attempt to change it. All the same, he was still feeling very nervous. He knew he'd feel a hundred times better as soon as he was in the saddle and heading as fast as possible for home. It would be as thrilling as going flat out for victory on the last lap of a moto-cross.

Now the lane flattened out and Lee pulled the bike across to the right and on to the plateau of moorland. Joanne showed him that her fingers were crossed as tightly as she could manage. She glanced behind her but could see nothing of Top-of-the-Moors Farm.

In the stillness of the morning the throaty roar of the engine as it came to life sounded deafening. Instinctively, Joanne swung round through 360 degrees to check whether anyone had been alerted. She expelled a long breath when she saw that they still had the landscape to themselves.

'Come on, come on, Jo!' he told her excitedly as he prepared to rocket away across the moor. 'I think we've made it! Fantastic!'

Even before she could settle on to the rear part of the seat Lee was accelerating through the gears. The old familiar sensations of speed and power and triumph came flooding back and suddenly it seemed to him that he and the bike had never been parted. When they were both at their peak, or just approaching it, they were one. He had always felt that; or, rather, he had felt it since the start of his success as a scrambler.

He was remembering the theory, so often proved to be true, that a motocross was won with a rapid start – and won in the first lap. Well, he'd made a

196

flying getaway from the lonely farmhouse and now he could see no obstacle ahead of them. Whatever use Mike Collier had made of the bike there was no doubt in Lee's mind that the young farmer had kept it in good shape. It felt as good as it had always done; the response when he shifted up a gear was immediate and electric. The ride home was a trip to be enjoyed.

The sudden eruption of earth on the skyline some distance away took Lee by surprise. A split second later he heard the heavy 'crump' of an explosion. Before he could decide what he should do another fountain of earth shot skywards several hundred metres to the right of the previous explosion; and this time the noise was much louder. Automatically, he swerved away to the left and reduced speed.

'What's going on?' he yelled over his shoulder.

Joanne was swallowing hard. Only a few moments earlier she had noticed the red flag fluttering lightly on one of the posts they'd sped past. At the time it hadn't occurred to her what it meant. But now she knew.

They were in the Army firing range; and they'd arrived while a deadly exercise was in progress.

'We've got to get out of here, Lee,' she shouted into his left ear. 'The Army have started a full-scale war or something with live ammunition. And we're on their land!'

He braked immediately, controlling the skidding

197

rear wheel with all his usual aplomb in spite of his astonishment at what he'd heard.

'But – aren't they supposed to let the public know before they start shooting?' he said. 'I mean –'

'They did,' she replied flatly. 'Red flags are flying on the boundary markers. I saw one some way back but I didn't think what it meant. Lee, we've just got to get away from here as fast as possible.'

'We can't go the way we've come,' he pointed out, 'because then we'd probably meet the Colliers searching like mad for the bike!'

As he spoke another explosion sent a column of earth and stones mushrooming into the sky: and this time the 'ker-rump' was a great deal louder.

'We'll go in that direction, away from the bombs,' Lee said decisively. He was thoroughly frightened, too, but he knew he had to control his fear if they were to escape. 'I expect they're mortars. They're not as bad as they look. Listen, I'm going to be riding at full chat, so sit tight. O.K.?'

She nodded as brightly as she could manage – and then braced herself for the surge of power as they started off again. On such springy terrain, the bounce was higher than she'd expected. Much as she'd have liked to put her arms round Lee's middle, she was determined not to: he had enough distractions as it was. The haversack was bumping a little on her shoulders, threatening to unbalance her, and she thought of getting rid of it. However, with the extra distance to be travelled they might after all need the spare fuel. By now the sun was well up and it was going to be a beautiful day. If, that was, they survived it. . . .

The land began to slip away to their left and Lee realised they were on the rim of a giant crater. On the lower slopes the vegetation was thicker and momentarily he thought of descending because surely they would be safer down there.

Then his eye was caught by a sudden movement away to their right. Cantering towards them was a uniformed figure on a horse. His first thought was that the man was coming to their aid: his second, that if they allowed themselves to be stopped and spoken to by any soldier, they'd be in trouble, if only for trespassing on Army land. Lee promptly swerved away to his left, down the slight slope under the rim and headed for a line of sturdy bushes that might screen them from a pursuer. In this kind of landscape he was in his element because it tested his skills as a scrambles rider.

Joanne hadn't noticed the horse and rider and so she supposed that Lee was simply using the crater as a temporary shelter. As they emerged from the bushes they neatly hurdled a narrow stream and then found themselves on a distinct pathway that appeared to meander along the side of the hollow. Lee decided they might as well follow it; with luck it would lead them away from the firing range – and the soldier on horseback. Soon they were climbing, though the gradient was only slight.

'Look, there's a man on a horse on the skyline!' Joanne called excitedly. 'We're safe!'

That wasn't Lee's reaction. In his eyes, the mounted soldier was almost as threatening as the explosions. Obviously, he was intending to cut off their escape. Lee realised he must have really galloped hard to reach that point on the rim of the crater so much ahead of them. But Lee had no intention of being caught. Deftly he changed gear, turned off the track and bumped over a tiny ridge of stones and rough ground. By now, Joanne had no option but to cling to him to prevent herself being bounced off the bike.

As he went through 180 degrees the bike began to slip on loose soil on the steep slope but Lee kept it going with a burst of power; and a final thrust enabled him to regain the pathway. But then, next instant, he was forced to skid to a halt.

For completely blocking the track was another soldier on horseback.

Lee felt utterly defeated. He would never have imagined that there would be *two* horsemen. Between them, they'd outflanked him. And now, right on cue, the other one was coming down the path towards them: a sergeant with a red band round his cap and riding a handsome chestnut. His eyes were as dark as gun barrels and for several moments he

200

simply stared at Lee and Joanne without saying a word.

'Were you trying to get yourselves killed, then?' he asked at last.

Lee tried to moisten his lips. 'We'd no idea when we set off that there was going to be shooting and bombs exploding.'

'And what do you think the red flags mean? Don't tell me you've never read the warning notices plastered up all over the place.'

'We didn't see them, er, until it was too late. But we were trying to get out of the way now. I've lost my way, that's all.'

Joanne wanted to help him out but she couldn't think of anything to say that would be of any use. Perhaps it would be best if she kept quiet – a silent admission of guilt might curb the sergeant's wrath. He had, she recognised, every right to be angry.

'You're joyriding, lad, that's what you're up to!' declared the sergeant savagely. 'And it could have been the last ride of *any sort* you'll ever have.'

'That's not true,' Lee retaliated spiritedly. 'We were recovering my motorcycle from the guy who stole it – that's why we're out here at this time of the morning.'

This time the sergeant chose to ignore what to him was a very obvious lie. He'd already sent a message through his walkie-talkie about the trespassers so that there would be a cease-fire until they'd been apprehended. But he didn't want to delay the resumption of the military exercise any longer than necessary. The kids had been stupid, criminally stupid, in his opinion, and had to be taught a lesson.

'If we hadn't been on patrol this morning and spotted you sneaking across our territory you probably *would* have been killed,' he now told them in a very cold, precise tone. His horse, which had been getting a little restive, suddenly became as stationary as a statue. It, too, had detected a change in the sergeant's mood. 'Now, I want you both off this land at the double – and we're going to follow to see that you do as you're told. But before you go Corporal Jackson here is going to take down your names and addresses and the names of your schools. Then your parents and head teachers will be hearing from my Commanding Officer. And I've no doubt the C.O. will recommend some proper punishment for your misconduct. Some good military discipline is what you two need.

'Right, Corporal, let's have their names in the book, then.'

Lee swallowed hard and gave his name and the other details demanded. It had occurred to him to provide a false name and address but he suspected the Military Police sergeant would have some means of double-checking his identity and thus an additional misdemeanour would simply result in a

202

more severe punishment eventually. When Joanne supplied her own details she added, defiantly, 'We're cousins, in case you're wondering.' But neither of the soldiers made any comment on that disclosure.

As soon as the corporal finished writing the sergeant began to issue instructions. It appeared that, after all, they weren't so very far from the boundary of the firing range and if they followed the track alongside the marker posts they'd come out on to a minor road that would lead them back to Lingdale Village. First, though, they were escorted out of the crater.

'Off you go, then,' said the sergeant after pointing out the marker posts on the skyline, 'and remember we shall be right behind you till you're off our territory. And just make sure you don't come back – ever – whether the red flags are flying or not. Then you won't be in danger of getting blown up.'

Within a few minutes they reached the road – and freedom. Lee had steeled himself not to look back; and, although he wasn't aware of it, of course, Joanne had done exactly the same. Now, though, Lee paused to express his profound relief at their escape.

'Honestly, I thought they were going to throw us straight into an Army prison camp or something! And even those horses looked as if they'd like to bite our heads off. Terrific size, weren't they?'

Joanne nodded eagerly. 'I don't think we have much luck with four-legged animals, you know. I mean, it was that blooming donkey that was the start of all our troubles, wasn't it?'

'You're right, Jo! I've always preferred two wheels to four legs. To start with, they're faster. Well, *these* wheels are. So, come on, let's speed off home. Then I can get down to the serious business of practising for the Inter-Club Championship races.'

Eight

'How is it, then?' Greg Shearsmith inquired, managing to produce a lop-sided grin as he spoke.

'Terrific – just as good as ever. I don't think that guy Collier messed it up at all but your Dad's an absolute miracle worker with the spanner,' Lee replied with unforced enthusiasm. 'I reckon my bike's in better shape than your face, Greg. Are you *really* sure you're fit enough to ride this afternoon?'

'Yeah, I'll be O.K. I've raced when I've had worse injuries than this one and *still* finished in the first three. I'm aiming to get my hands on that winged trophy for the Best Rider in the Championship, so one little knock on the head isn't going to stop me. No way!'

Lee shrugged and turned away to make some apparent adjustment to a cable. He owed a considerable debt to the Shearsmith family and so he didn't want to say too much. It was typical of Greg to be so dismissive about a personal injury but Lee

205

suspected that this one was just as bad as it looked; it had happened while Greg, attempting as usual to take a near-impossible jump in spectacular fashion, had crashed during a private practice session. Of course, a facial injury wouldn't be obvious during the Championships when he was properly helmeted but his fitness to ride in a fierce competition at speed was surely in doubt. That was particularly so at Terncliff, one of the toughest courses any of the Skalbrooke riders had ever seen.

It had been constructed on a wooded hill that resembled, as Graham Relton, Skalbrooke's captain, had put it, 'the side of a Swiss mountain – and the *steepest* side at that!' Because of a continuing lack of rain the terrain was exceptionally dry and, during practice that morning, clouds of red dust had risen skywards.

All the same, it was a track Lee was eager to test his skills on at racing speed: the jumps and tight turns on the downhill stretches were exactly what he'd been practising at the start of the season. Perhaps, he'd been reflecting, his luck had changed at last. He'd been selected as one of Skalbrooke's six top riders for the Intermediates and had he been allowed to choose his own course for the Championship he'd have picked Terncliff. Even Uncle Ken was smiling at him again (though, of course, it was too much to expect that he had ousted Darren as their uncle's favourite). Apparently Uncle Ken had actually enjoyed his visit to Top-of-the-Moors Farm, according to Joanne who'd lost no time in relating the known details to Lee. Mr Wragby had gone to the farm to 'wipe the floor' with Mike Collier and his family, and, seemingly, had done just that most effectively. As predicted, young Collier had protested that he'd just found the bike and was intending to hand it over to the police when he had time. As a result of Uncle Ken's threats, however, it was unlikely Collier would lay his hands on anyone else's machine ever again. 'Dad loves a good scrap, especially when he knows he's going to win by a knock-out,' Jo concluded her report. 'Oh yes, and he was quite impressed with the way you – and I, she says modestly – located the bike and got it back all on our own. I suspect he knows Darren wouldn't have managed such a feat.'

Lee now glanced across the paddock to where his brother was standing with Uncle Ken. Daz had said very little about Lee's success in retrieving his bike and Lee supposed that Daz was a bit worried about the resumption of their rivalry on the racetrack. Even though both were officially riding for Skalbrooke against the best scramblers from other clubs it was inevitable that the brothers would be equally determined to finish ahead of each other, whatever their fate overall. Moreover, Lee hadn't forgiven Daz for his hurtful remarks during the period he thought he'd lost his bike for ever.

Quite a crowd was gathering round a boy called Duncan McGlew, a Scot who had only recently joined the Terncliff Club and brought with him a reputation for high speed and high skills on grass tracks. Duncan, a remarkably thin, wiry boy with a mane of carroty hair, seemed to have collected a sizeable personal fan club already and he'd been pointed out to Lee by another rider the moment he appeared on the scene.

'From the way he's been going in practice, they think it's going to be a case of Duncan-first-and-where-are-the-rest?' related Nathan Pike, a member of the neighbouring Rockleigh Youth Motorcycle Club and also one of the fancied competitors in the Intermediates.

'Well, if you make sure you put him out of the race I'll look after the others, Nat,' Lee replied with a grin. He rather liked the Rockleigh rider who concealed a fierce determination to win under a gentle, often amused, manner. 'Then you and I can finish first and second.'

'Just as long as *I* am first and *you* are second,' Nathan responded. 'Though I won't object if you're only a wheel-length behind at the line – it'll make it look as though you're *nearly* as good as me!'

There was no time to continue that sort of conversation because the Juniors were on the last lap of their race and so the Intermediates were rolling up to the starting line. Just as Lee was about to pull down his goggles Uncle Ken hurried across for a final word.

'All the best, Lee. I'll be shouting for you all the way. So have a great ride.'

Lee nodded his thanks. He was glad his helmet must conceal the surprise he felt. Normally Uncle Ken had time only for words with Daz. Perhaps, Lee reflected, his uncle was trying to make up for the absence of Joanne who hadn't been able to avoid accompanying her mother on a shopping trip to London. He missed Jo more than he would admit; but, after all, she had shared most of his adventures and successes and she seemed to bring him luck.

The blue haze above the line of exhausts thickened as engines were revved again and again. All eyes, of course, were on the taut tape that would spring sideways to signal the start. Darren, in his distinctive black-and-yellow helmet, had lined up next to his brother. He, like every other rider, was praying for a brilliant getaway and a real chance to prove that he was the Tiger of the Track he so often imagined himself to be.

Greg Shearsmith, striving to get a flier, nudged under the tape, got a severe reprimand from the starter and had to be hauled back more than a metre by his father. As always, the ebony Shearsmith Special was in immaculate condition. Harry Shearsmith, though, had given every bit as much attention to Lee Parnaby's green-and-silver machine and Lee knew that if he failed to win the race it wouldn't be for mechanical reasons.

The tension had crept into Lee's shoulders and he could feel the tightness in muscles at the base of the neck. Like every other ambitious rider, he was affected by nerves as the countdown began before a race; but this event, his first Inter-Club Championship, was a very special occasion. He was determined to make it a memorable one.

Because he was close to the starter's left hand he sensed the movement a fraction of a second before the elastic catapulted out of sight.

The race was on!

Lee's initial acceleration was superbly timed. He'd made the fast start he'd prayed for – and yet, amazingly, Duncan McGlew was ahead of him. Somehow the boy a newspaper had inevitably dubbed 'The Flying Scot' had seized the initiative and was already hurtling towards the first downhill turn with Lee as his nearest rival.

For two of the riders there was disaster even before that left-hander was reached. A Yamaha in the hands of a boy who'd become too throttle-happy in his anxiety to get a flier reared almost like a rocket; and a Terncliff rider alongside him, swerving to avoid a wavering Honda, crashed straight into the Yamaha's fork as it came down. Momentarily the starter thought of stopping the race because it seemed that the fallen pair must be badly hurt. Parents and other helpers, however, were already on the track and rapidly sorting out the trouble. Nonetheless, both riders were too shaken to continue.

Unaware, of course, of what was going on behind him, Lee went in pursuit of the green-helmeted McGlew, blasting confidently over the first jump and then bouncing easily over a rib-like series of half-exposed roots. The pace was the hottest most of the spectators had ever witnessed.

Lee was thankful to have made such a great start but he was keen to know how far he was ahead of such obvious rivals as Graham Relton, Nat Pike and Greg Shearsmith. Because the course was downhill and without a sharp turn for almost a hundred metres he had no way of knowing where the rest were. He would have liked to sneak a glance over his shoulder but he knew that could be fatal.

McGlew, welded to sheer speed like every other grass track racer, seemed set to establish a new record for a Terncliff lap. His lead was already substantial and the exhilarated crowd was plainly on the side of the Flying Scot as he zipped round the treacherous first hairpin. He took it so well that some spectators actually applauded, an almost un-heard of compliment at that stage of a race. Lee, following in his wheel-tracks and straining to see through the mushrooming dust, had his engine screaming in third as he attempted to slice into Duncan's lead.

Graham Relton, who'd suffered in the congestion at the first turn, was pushing against Nathan Pike for third position. It was unusual for Graham to be anywhere but out in front but for once he'd not made the best of starts. The top Skalbrooke trophy winner, he was always realistic about his riding and he wouldn't blame his bike for his present position. He knew his concentration had lapsed a fraction at the start. But that only made him all the more determined to make up the lost ground as quickly as possible. His supporters would think he was unwell if he wasn't soon in the lead!

Nat was just as positive in his approach and he wasn't going to yield so much as a centimetre to the Skalbrooke champion. So, for the moment, Nat was more concerned with keeping Graham at bay than with overtaking the pair ahead of him. To Nat, motocross was a tactical exercise, not a fairground brawl.

The four leaders had drawn well clear of the rest of the field, who were bunching up dangerously. Greg Shearsmith, for one, was feeling particularly frustrated as he tried to break out of the pack. But the two riders directly in front of him were adopting a cautious policy in the dusty conditions of this fast, switchback course. Alongside him, the self-styled Tiger of the Track was also snarling furiously at not being able to make the progress he knew was necessary at this stage. The sight of his brother so far ahead of him already was tormenting Darren Parnaby.

Lee, trying to keep an eye on Duncan's rear wheel, was oblivious now to what was going on anywhere else in the race. As he went banshee-ing round another sharply rising curve into a thickly wooded zone he calculated that his best chance of catching Duncan would be on the straight at the very top of the course where both the starting and finishing points were located. Moreover, that was where the biggest crowds would be and Lee relished the thought of having a good audience at the moment he went into the lead. But it wasn't going to happen on this first lap. The Scot was still too far in front for that. Lee silently urged himself on to greater effort. By now he had total faith in the performance of his machine. It had all the reliability and power he needed. So everything now depended on his own skills and determination – plus, perhaps, a little bit of luck.

To many spectators, it seemed that the only questions to be answered were a) which of the first two at present would be the winner; and b) which of the next pair would finish third. The rest seemed out of it already. But then, suddenly, dramatically, the race was thrown wide open again.

Towards the back of the pack two club-mates

who had been fighting out a personal duel went for the same narrow gap simultaneously. The collision was as violent as it was inevitable. As the bikes bounced away from each other, toppling over as they did so, they mowed down other riders like scythes.

The calamity occurred on a downhill stretch that was just tightening into a severe turn. Spectators were gathered there in strength. Instinctively, several people leapt on to the track to tend the injured and drag the fallen bikes out of the way. Seconds later, just as a yellow flag was being raised to indicate trouble, Duncan McGlew was tearing down to the same spot. His record speed that had almost enabled him to lap some of his rivals was now the cause of his own disaster.

Desperately The Flying Scot tried to brake and slide his machine round the first obstacle. But his grass track skills were no help to him in that minefield of bikes and bodies. Duncan crunched over a horizontal front wheel and pitched head first into a bush. For him, the race was over.

Lee, who'd been barely a couple of lengths adrift of the leader, glimpsed a white flag bearing a red cross. As his brain recorded that medical aid was needed for someone he tried to jink his machine between the scattering people and the litter of bikes and equipment. His strength and ability to weave at speed very nearly enabled him to get through

unscathed. But just as he attempted a gear change on the acute, rising corner, his front wheel struck an abandoned helmet; he tried to twist away but the manoeuvre caused the bike to fall over sideways. Lee just managed to get his left leg free of the frame as it came down; so he landed on his stern. In the drama of the moment he didn't even feel the pain of the bump. His only concern was that his engine should be all right.

With both leaders on the deck Nathan Pike seized his heaven-sent opportunity. Sensibly he'd slowed down on seeing the carnage ahead of him and was prepared to pick his way through it to freedom. Graham Relton, not used at all to being behind at this stage of a race, shot past Nat as he slowed down. And Graham duly paid the penalty he deserved to pay for such impetuousness. A boy who was stumbling off the track crossed his path, Graham swerved, couldn't correct in time – and slid sideways into the bush that had already claimed Duncan McGlew.

That was the moment when the race might have been called off – but, fortunately for the eventual winner, no official took that decision to hoist a red flag.

In addition to Nat, two other riders managed to improve their positions to great effect. But while Darren Parnaby threaded himself and his machine through the middle of the disaster area with commendable care Greg Shearsmith zoomed off round the perimeter and didn't even notice that he'd tangled with a marker tape at one point. Both Daz and Greg then went off in pursuit of the clear leader, Nathan Pike.

Lee, meanwhile, was reunited with his bike. To his delight, it seemed to be in perfect shape and the engine was still running sweetly. He wasn't even aware of his own bruises. A lot of ground had been lost but at least he was still in the race – and there weren't many of the starters who could say that.

Thankfully, he chased after his brother and Greg and the new, outright leader, Nathan Pike.

In spite of having been on the floor, Lee was still a long way ahead of those of the rest of the field who'd missed the great pile-up. So the race really concerned only the four riders now strung out in Indian file. Nathan believed that as long as he took no unwise risks he would keep the lead until the end; his chief worry had been the skill and flair of Lee Parnaby, the rider for whom he had the greatest respect. Nat hadn't expected Duncan to stay on two wheels on such a course and he was right. He was sure the greatest challenge would come from Lee – and now he had seen Lee, too, tumble into oblivion.

Greg, currently in third place, was determined to get the better of Darren, who was only just ahead of him. Patience had never been one of his qualities

217

and throughout the next lap he tried everything he knew to overtake. He was prepared to ride to the limit to win that winged trophy. But he wasn't aware that fate had already dealt him a fatal blow. For when he took an outside route round the disaster zone the tape he'd crossed had snapped and a length of it had wrapped itself around his rear brake mechanism. So, continuously, it was pulling on the brake. Even Greg's abundant strength wasn't able to cope with that problem as he tried to conjure more power from his engine. He was beginning to feel exhausted and he assumed his old head injury was taking its toll of him.

On the next downhill section Greg made a last, superhuman effort to bury Daz, as he thought of the tactic. The still gleaming Shearsmith Special soared from a ramp alongside the startled Darren; it seemed certain to overtake him but the split-second the rear wheel touched down the Special's brake locked immovably. There was a violent swerve and Greg was flung bodily across the track as the bike plunged end over end, and very spectacularly, into the banking.

Daz could hardly believe his luck. *Everything* was working out in his favour. And, because he was thinking that, his concentration wavered at just the wrong moment. On the next downhill jump which followed immediately, he failed to keep his weight at the back. Thus, on landing, the handle-bars seemed to rise up into his chest with the force of a hammer blow. Darren was badly winded. For the next hundred metres or so he thought he'd never get his breath back. In one sense he didn't, because in struggling to breathe properly he lost control of his machine.

Quite gently, he slid from the machine to the track. Fortunately he'd given up at the very spot where Uncle Ken was stationed; and within moments Mr Wragby himself had removed his elder nephew from the place of danger.

Almost before Daz was clear of the track Lee was zooming past the same spot. Nothing could have

heartened him more than the events of the last minute or so. From fourth position he'd improved to second without any extra effort on his own part. Now he could concentrate totally on catching Nat Pike and then winning the race.

As leader, Nathan was less happy than he'd care to admit. He knew he could judge the pace better when coming from behind. A glance back on one of the hairpin turns had shown him that Lee Parnaby was his nearest pursuer; and Lee, he knew, would push him all the way. Nat sensed that if Lee were given even half a chance of overtaking then he would seize it like a greyhound catching a hare.

Lee was reducing the distance between them metre by metre. It was his technique at the downhill jumps that was giving him the advantage. Well as Nat was riding, he hadn't the flair to get away so speedily from those obstacles. All the same, Nathan refused to be rattled by anything. His nerve had been good in the past and it wasn't going to fail him now.

As they went into the last lap Nathan was still just about a length in front. Twice on that final circuit Lee tried desperately to overtake immediately after a jump. Each time Nathan, with the benefit of being able to choose the shortest route, closed the gap.

Even so, when they at last regained the finishing straight, Lee, pulling wide of his rival, managed to

produce a final surge of power. Together the two riders flashed past the chequered flag.

The judge himself couldn't separate them. He declared the race to be the first dead-heat he'd known in his career.

'That was tremendous, Lee, tremendous,' he said after congratulating both riders. 'And all the more amazing because you were on the floor at one stage! Didn't think it was possible for you to get up again after that, let alone ride such a finish!'

Lee had never been happier. He knew he'd never ridden a better race in his life; only bad luck had prevented him from being the outright winner.

'Well done, Nat,' he said, slapping his friend and rival on the back. 'But I'm telling you this now; next time, I'm going to have first place *all to myself.*'

MICHAEL HARDCASTLE

Tiger of the Track

One

As he trudged up the lane from the church towards
Terson's Fields, the shortest route home, Lee Parnaby was mentally reviewing his performance on the
track that afternoon. He was well aware that he
hadn't been riding in top form, or anything like it.
True, he'd improved with each race, finishing third
to Nathan Pike and Greg Shearsmith in the third and
last event. But he knew he should have won that race
for he'd been the outright leader with under two laps
to go. Then, when he'd slowed to avoid a straggler
who was toppling from his machine, Nathan had
seized the opportunity to overtake. Greg, with furious determination, had snatched second place practically on the finishing line.

Lee was carrying two helmets, his own and his
brother Darren's. Now, as he remembered how sick
he'd felt at the start of the first race, he banged them
against his thigh in renewed annoyance with himself.
He felt he deserved to be punished! Five minutes

before the race began he'd eaten a particularly gooey chocolate bar, not to calm his nerves but simply to provide extra energy. As a fitness and diet fanatic, he should have known better. Because of a sudden whim, he'd gone completely against his own reasoning. With the inevitable pre-match tension already affecting his nervous system at that point, it was no wonder he'd felt like throwing up just as the starter released the tape.

What made things even worse, as far as he was concerned, was that Darren had won that race. It was his first outright triumph for several weeks and, predictably, he'd made the most of it, boasting to all and sundry that he was definitely on his way to becoming the Champion rider of his class in the Skalbrooke Schoolboy Motorcycle Club. Naturally, he'd laughed at Lee's failure to finish among the leaders, adding that top class motocross wasn't the sport for weaklings like his little brother.

Lee was well used to such insults from Daz (the nickname Darren himself relished because he claimed it stood for 'Dazzling'). Darren was the elder by exactly one year and one day and he always made the most of that advantage. For Lee, even his birthday was usually something of an anti-climax; all the celebrating had taken place the previous day. Lee felt he was always placed second in just about everything and so he was, in his own view, a second class citizen of sorts. His mother tried to insist that he had parity in all things with Darren, but Lee knew it simply wasn't true. Daz came first in age and first in nearly everything else that happened in their family life. 'That,' Darren chortled, 'is an elder brother's privilege.' Well, Lee was determined that situation shouldn't exist in the field of sport. In fact, there really wasn't much between them in terms of success to date; and thus the rivalry was invariably intense.

Near the end of the lane Lee ducked under a hedge to take a short cut. By crossing the corner of a wheat-field he could save a couple of hundred metres before reaching the path that led to the new housing-estate. But as he emerged from the hedge a stray branch knocked one of the helmets from his grasp.

It was Daz's black-and-yellow striped helmet that was on the ground and, for a moment, Lee thought of leaving it there. He shouldn't have had to carry it home for its owner in the first place. It was typical of Darren that he'd blithely expected Lee to look after his equipment for him. Actually, Lee supposed that Daz had just forgotten to pick it up himself before going off on a fishing-expedition with some of his cronies. But anyone else would have taken care to see that his favourite helmet was put in a safe place, not left in a corner of Harry Shearsmith's transporter. Described by his son Greg as 'an absolute genius with the old tuning-up tools', Mr Shearsmith generously also looked after the mechanical side of Lee's racing-bike. The Shearsmiths had given Lee a lift, dropping him in Lingdale Village, near the church.

As he picked up the distinctive, wasp-coloured helmet it occurred to him that he had never tried it on. He grinned at the notion that, if the helmet fitted Daz's swollen head, it certainly wouldn't fit his own, which was a perfectly normal size. To his considerable surprise, it really fitted quite snugly. If he hadn't known otherwise, he would have supposed that Darren's inflated ego was shrinking at last.

He decided he might as well keep it on for a while. Carrying two helmets wasn't easy, especially when he was also burdened with the American footballer-style padded protector, now in need of a minor repair, which he wore to save his shoulders in race-spills. It was still a fairly warm day and he thought, a trifle enviously, of the coolness of the river where Darren was likely to be fishing. On the other hand, that wasn't a sport (if such it was, he reflected) that appealed to Lee in any way at all.

He'd just reached the perimeter of the field and was within a few strides of the well-worn path leading to the first group of houses when the attack was launched. There wasn't an advance warning of any kind as someone tackled him, rugby-fashion, round the knees.

Lee hadn't a hope of staying on his feet. As a motocrosser, he was used to falls: he knew how to cope with them. But this time, when he hit the ground and tried to roll clear of trouble, he was

230

unable to free his legs. Then, as he struggled to break away from his attacker, he received a fierce blow – he didn't know whether it was a punch or a kick – in the ribs.

The pain was awful. Somehow, though, he pulled his legs from his attacker's grasp. Just as he was turning on his side he saw a punch coming – but too fast for him to avoid it. It landed in the region of his solar plexus and doubled him up completely as the breath was knocked out of him. For a few moments he thought he was going to die. And he still hadn't seen who was attacking him. He was sure he was being mugged, and he couldn't begin to imagine why it was happening to him.

Dimly, he heard someone giving an order. 'Put him on his back, and keep him there. Yeah, go on, put your foot on his arms. That's it, both of 'em.'

The torture-zones suddenly shifted. Pain now flared in his forearms as they were stamped into the ground – ground that was unyielding after weeks without rain. The only possible relief for Lee was that the feet pinning him down were wearing trainers, not shoes or, even worse, boots. The position alone was humiliating and he was utterly helpless.

To make matters marginally worse, the sun was in his eyes when he was able to open them. So, at first, he couldn't make out who his attackers were. All he knew was that there were two of them. Then, gradually, his vision improved. He looked up at the boys who were staring down at him and recognised them immediately. Pete Webster and Simmy Roddick were pupils at his own school but a year ahead of him. But, so far as he could remember, he'd never had anything to do with either of them at any time.

'Get that stupid helmet off him, Simmy. I want him to hear every word I've got to say to him. Hear everything as clear as a bell.'

The speaker was just beyond Lee's view but he knew that voice. It belonged to Andy Haylin, the school's best-known bully and a regular tormentor of younger boys. Haylin had a certain claim to fame because his father was a former professional wrestler who had appeared in a number of televised bouts. Andy was forever boasting that he was going to be more famous than his father (which wouldn't be much of an achievement as Haylin senior had never been better than a third-rate performer and nowadays rarely worked at all). He collected cronies, and then discarded them, with the regularity that other boys started fashionable new hobbies. Fairly obviously, Webbo and Roddick, a particularly dim youth in Lee's opinion, were Haylin's latest henchmen.

Roddick, without shifting his weight from Lee's left arm, bent down and removed the striped helmet. Inevitably, he took the opportunity to bang Lee's head on the ground in the process.

'Hey!' he exclaimed in plain astonishment. 'It isn't him, Andy. It's his kid brother!'

232

That revelation brought Haylin directly into Lee's line of improved vision so that he could see for himself that Simmy Roddick wasn't just being dimmer than ever. The hefty Haylin scowled down at his victim and for a long interval didn't utter a word.

'Come on, let me get up!' Lee yelled. 'You've just admitted you've got the wrong guy. So –'

'Shut up!' Haylin thundered. 'I give the orders. You're just dirt on the floor. You haven't been dealt with yet.'

Webster, the silent one, reinforced his leader's anger by pressing harder on Lee's arm and twisting his heel at the same time. Lee couldn't prevent himself crying out with pain. If they went on like this they were going to break an arm. Then he wouldn't be able to ride his motor-cycle for weeks, perhaps months. He vowed not to struggle any further while such odds were stacked against him. Haylin and his thugs were capable of almost any rottenness, so he lay still and hoped they would admit he wasn't worth bothering with any longer.

'He's just as bad as their Darren,' volunteered Roddick, sensing his leader's mood. 'They both ride around on those flashy motor-bikes, knocking people out of the way. So this one deserves it just as much as the other.'

'Look, I haven't done anything,' Lee protested quietly. 'If you've got a quarrel with my brother then settle it with him. Be fair!'

234

Andy Haylin ignored that plea as he ignored everything that was different from his own point of view. It didn't really bother him that he'd made a mistake. Instead of delivering his message to Darren Parnaby, personally, he could send it just as well through his kid brother. In any case, he could always fix Darren another time.

Ponderously he moved forward one step, so that he was standing almost directly above Lee's chest. For Lee, it was rather like staring up at a bulging towerblock from a ground-floor entrance. From that position Haylin really did seem quite threatening instead of, as usual, simply fat and unpleasant.

'This is my message – not a message, no, a *warning* – a warning to your ugly big brother and you as well,' he said as heavily as he could manage. 'In future, leave Garry Talbot alone. Never get in his way again. Just don't interfere with him in any way. Get it?'

Lee hadn't the faintest notion what he was talking about. He didn't think he'd ever heard of anyone called Garry Talbot. So presumably he was a character in Daz's year at school.

'You and your brother will suffer a lot worse than this – *ten times* worse – if there's any more trouble about Garry,' he said emphatically. 'Right, get off his arms now so he can get up.'

His minions dutifully stepped aside. Lee closed his eyes in relief as the pressure on his arms was removed. However, it was several moments before he felt able

235

to try to get to his feet. Haylin and his gang stood and watched him. Then, just as Lee started to lever himself upwards Andy Haylin uttered a final reminder.

'This is just so's you won't forget, Parnaby.'

He drew back his right foot and then drove the toe-cap viciously into Lee's chest. Whereupon he turned, nodded to his cronies to follow him, and walked away towards the estate. None of them looked back even once.

Lee was doubled up with the agony of that final attack. His entire upper body felt as if it had been tangling with a car-crusher for several rounds. It was hard even to breathe properly. He held his left hand tight against the rib-cage: he was sure at least one rib must have been cracked. No fall from a motor-cycle had ever caused him such pain as this.

After what seemed like an hour, but in truth was only a few minutes, he made himself stand upright. The sweat that beaded his forehead wasn't brought on by the heat of the day. Lee would have given a lot for a drink of cold water. He thought of calling at the nearest house but then he dismissed the idea. For all he knew, Haylin or Roddick might live there. That would be just his luck on such a day.

With both arms wrapped round his chest he forced himself to walk as normally as possible through the estate. Fortunately for him, he encountered no one he knew. He received one or two strange or sympathetic looks from householders in their gardens but nobody addressed a word to him. He was thankful about that. He still didn't know how he was going to manage when he reached home.

By then, however, he'd already rehearsed exactly what he was going to say to Darren.

Two

He'd hoped to be able to get into the house and up to his room without anyone knowing he was home. His luck, though, was still completely out. His mother came round the corner of the house, her arms full of the roses she'd been cutting, just as Lee sidled up the drive.

'I thought you were going to be back early,' Mrs Parnaby greeted him with a frown. His heart sank still further. For some reason, she was in a bad mood.

'I just got held up. Sorry.' It was slightly easier to talk than he'd expected. All the same, he desperately wanted to go and lie down. Then the pain might start to ebb away. Rest was always recommended for injuries: he'd heard one sports physio claim it was the best medicine of all. But there was something he needed to know first. 'Is Darren back, then?'

'No. But he told me he was going to be late, so I didn't have to worry about his tea.'

She'd been studying him as she spoke and now her

238

eyes really narrowed. 'Have you fallen off and injured yourself, Lee?'

He shook his head vehemently. 'Of course not! We were only practising today, anyway.'

'Have you been fighting, then? Getting yourself into trouble?'

'Definitely not!'

He rather wished that he could say he had been in a fight for then he would at least have struck a blow or two in self-defence.

'Well, from the way you're standing, you've been up to something unhealthy. Still, it's a good thing you're fit because I've got some gardening jobs for you to finish off tonight as you're the only man about the house.'

This time he could let out a groan that would serve a double purpose. He always got the rotten jobs because his father was away at sea and Daz cunningly avoided being around when there was domestic work to do.

'Look, Mum, I think I'll go and have a bath – I feel a bit hot and sticky.'

'Wonders,' she exclaimed, managing a half-smile, 'never cease. . . .'

He was just disappearing into the house when she called him back.

'Oh, you've got to ring Joanne. She's got some very exciting news for you. She rang you ten minutes ago when you should have been here.'

Lee did his best not to look exasperated. 'I'll give her a buzz after my bath. I –'

'No! Now! This minute! That girl's kindness itself so far as you're concerned and I'm not letting you be unkind in return by keeping her waiting.'

The pain in his side wasn't any better by the time he got indoors but he rid himself of some of his frustrations by slinging Darren's helmet, as fiercely as he could manage, into the base of the cupboard by the wall-phone. It would have pleased him immensely if the helmet had split clean in two: but of course it didn't. Scramblers' helmets were designed to withstand all manner of misuse. His own gear he took up to his room, the room he still unhappily shared with his brother, and stowed it away out of Daz's indiscriminate reach. When Daz needed something in a hurry he didn't care whose possessions he seized.

Before going down to telephone he considered running his bath: but then he decided he would need the water as hot as possible to soothe away his agony. Just now and again Joanne could be very talkative indeed. In any case, the urgent bath would be a good excuse for cutting short the conversation. Joanne was his cousin, a year younger than himself and often his staunch ally against Darren, whom she considered to be boastful. It was her father, Ken Wragby, who had provided Darren and Lee with their motocross machines and supported them at meetings. However,

240

Uncle Ken had always favoured Darren and Joanne resented that as much as Lee. It was one of the reasons why Lee was content to accept so much help from the Shearsmiths, even though Greg Shearsmith was actually as deadly a rival as Darren in Lee's estimation.

'What's this exciting news then?' Lee asked without preliminaries when he got through to Joanne.

'The best in the world, Lee! Dad's bought ME a motor-bike as a late, late birthday present. And he says I can race it at the special Bank Holiday meeting on Monday. So I'll be flat out to beat you and Daz – oh, and everybody else as well in the Intermediates. Terrific, isn't it!'

'Oh sure, great.'

There was a pause before Joanne spoke again. 'Well, thanks for sounding so pleased for me. I sure appreciate it.'

'I said it was great, didn't I? What do you want me to do, imitate an Indian war-whoop or something?'

'O.K., Lee, I get the message: you've got more important things on your mind. Want to fill me in about them? Or are they for boys only?'

'Look, I've had a rotten day,' he mumbled. 'I've got to go and have a bath now.'

'Gosh, things must *really* be bad!' she laughed. 'Did you fall in a mud –'

'Don't you start!' he snarled and slammed down the receiver.

241

Two minutes later, he stretched out full-length in the bath to get maximum benefit from a good soak, and thought about Joanne. Apart from being his cousin she was a good friend and they'd had some marvellous times together. He had no doubt at all that she'd be a fine competitor as a scrambles-rider. Many times she'd demonstrated her control, her mastery in fact, of a machine. She should have been allowed to compete years earlier but her father didn't believe that girls and bikes went together. She was his only child and that was one of the reasons why he'd devoted so much attention to Darren and Lee. Yet he'd often seen for himself at Skalbrooke meetings how determined and successful some of the girls could be in even the most difficult racing conditions. After all, girls didn't get any concessions just because they were girls.

Lee knew that Jo would revel in the opportunity to show what she could do as a motocrosser. She'd yearned for this chance without ever trying to put undue pressure on her father. Now that Uncle Ken had presented her with a bike it was no wonder that Jo was so thrilled she wanted to share the news immediately with her best friend (because that's what Lee was, as she'd told him, albeit a little diffidently, the last time they'd been together). Lee couldn't help feeling guilty at the way he'd treated her on the phone. On the other hand, she had an annoying habit of being flippant just when he wanted to be serious. It

242

was time she tried to understand his real feelings for once.

He supposed she wouldn't be in a jokey mood on Monday. She'd have to think very hard about how to ride her first race as a member of the Skalbrooke Club. Of one thing there was no doubt: she would be out to win so, on that basis, Joanne would be his rival, not his friend or his cousin. Friendship counted for nothing at all when the starting-tape sprang aside and everyone roared into the first bend, determined to establish a prime position for the long race ahead. If anything, family ties simply added bite to the competition. Certainly that was so in the case of Darren and himself. Except that, with them, the urge to defeat the other was as deep as a mine-shaft.

Lee shifted his position in the bath and, as he did so, experienced another sharp stab of pain in his side. Gingerly he explored the area again and was convinced that he could feel a gap in one of his ribs. So he had broken it after all! He groaned. He couldn't help himself. What on earth was he going to do now? Perhaps he should go and see his doctor or present himself as a casualty at the local hospital? But if he did that, and an X-ray revealed a fracture, he'd be banned from riding, probably for weeks. Life wouldn't be worth living if that happened. Daz would never stop crowing about his feebleness. Joanne wouldn't spare him any sympathy. She'd be too busy building her own reputation as a rider. His ambition to become the

243

top points' scorer in the Intermediates' group would disappear in a blue cloud of someone else's exhaust smoke. All because Daz had stupidly fallen foul of some thugs and . . .

Lee sat up sharply: and then, rather more carefully, got to his feet. He was beginning to wallow in self-pity and that was no good at all. He must be positive in everything he did as he'd told himself umpteen times before the start of the current moto-cross year.

As he dried himself his fingers instinctively returned to the rib-cage. This time he couldn't quite detect that ominous gap, though the area was still painful to touch. Maybe it was only deep bruising after all – and that shouldn't prevent his riding as usual. The soaking must have done him some good after all: and now he towelled the rest of himself quite vigorously.

He could even contemplate enjoying a meal. But he was determined to avoid those gardening jobs.

Lee was asleep, and had been in bed for nearly an hour, when Darren came in. As usual, he didn't care how much noise he made as he closed their bedroom-door. Lee blinked against the glare of the light over Darren's bed. He turned on his side: and once again the pain in his ribs caused him to cry out.

'Dreaming about another of your terrible crashes on the track?' Daz jeered when he realised that his

younger brother was awake. 'Must be like a continuous nightmare if you keep thinking about *all* the mistakes you keep making on that puny machine of yours!'

Lee managed to raise himself on one elbow and the pain receded a little. He didn't want to get into another futile slanging match with Daz but he had to say something. He'd already suffered enough on Darren's account for one day.

'What did you do to Garry Talbot?' he asked quietly but firmly.

Darren, who was just stepping out of his jeans, paused with one leg out and one leg in. He looked both foolish and non-plussed at the same time.

'What's that got to do with you?' he retaliated when he was able to speak.

'Plenty! But only because of what you've done. So, come on, give.'

Darren still hesitated, even though he recognised, from the intensity of Lee's manner, how important the question was to him. Instinctively, Daz was calculating how much he might lose by answering it truthfully.

'He's that fat little squirt who got in my way at the last race meeting,' he admitted at last. 'Actually, he did it twice, the stupid jerk. They should never have let him on the track.'

Lee had only the vaguest recollection of the boy. 'But what did you *do* to him?'

'Nothing at all, really,' Darren replied with a shrug and then continued his undressing. 'I told you: he got in my way twice when I wanted to lap him. Just dawdling along at the tail of the field, slap bang in the middle of the track, so I had to shift him. I put my foot into him and pushed him off his beat-up old bike.'

Darren paused and then laughed at the recollection: 'He's so feeble he didn't even have his helmet on properly. It fell off when he went down. You should have seen his face when he hit the dirt – looked like he was going to cry buckets! I saw him after racing but he didn't dare say a word to me. Knew he was totally in the wrong, I expect. In fact, now I think about it, I should have forced him to apologise.'

By Darren's usual standards when encountering interference during a race, the treatment meted out to Garry Talbot was quite mild. Certainly Lee couldn't understand why the boy should have called in the services of Andy Haylin for the purpose of revenge.

'Where's Talbot come from? I never saw him before the last meeting. He's not at our school, is he?' Lee asked.

Darren shook his head and then did a very neat backward flip on to his bed. He liked to give the impression that he was athletic. The truth was quite different: he avoided all physical exercise whenever possible. It was his often-stated belief that so long as a rider possessed brains one didn't have to be particularly fit to win at motocross. In his opinion, he had an abundance of brain power.

'His father runs that new leisure centre the other side of Lingdale,' he revealed, pulling the single sheet up under his chin. 'His old man probably pushed Gallopless Garry into motocross to get extra publicity for the centre. Didn't realise the kid's too scared to go fast enough to keep up even with tail-enders. Anyway, like I said, what's all this got to do with you, little brother? Has he been pleading with you to ask me to be kind to him in future? No chance! Next time

247

I'll ride right over him, squash him into the earth like a fat worm. That's where he belongs.'

'If you do that, then Andy Haylin and his private army of thugs will take YOU apart – bone by bone,' Lee told him. He had the satisfaction of seeing that Daz was suitably startled. 'It'd've happened to you today if they hadn't mistaken me for you because I was wearing your rotten helmet. So I got the beating up instead. It was supposed to be a warning to you to leave Talbot alone in future. He's either paying for protection or Haylin owes him a favour. Either way, you'll definitely suffer if you touch him again.'

Darren had the decency to inquire how much Lee had been hurt but he didn't offer any sympathy. He was, he swore, just as puzzled as Lee as to why Andy Haylin had gone to such lengths on Talbot's behalf. But he'd find out what it was all about at the meeting on Monday.

'What were you doing wearing *my* helmet?' he asked aggressively.

'Doing you a favour, that's what!' was the spirited reply. 'You'd forgotten it and like an idiot I carried it home for you. Then, just because I tried it on for a laugh, I got attacked. I think Haylin's kick smashed one of my ribs. Hurts every time I move a muscle.'

He could have predicted that would make Daz laugh – and it did.

'That's because you're soft, really soft,' he added. 'You think you're tough but you're not. That's why you always hang around with girls like Joanne. You're not man enough to be one of the boys, *little* brother!'

And on that note he triumphantly switched out his bed-light.

'Get lost!' Lee yelled into the darkness. 'That's total rubbish.'

After that, neither of them spoke again that night. It was a very long time, though, before Lee managed to get to sleep again. Two thoughts kept chasing through his mind: one concerned Daz's remark about his friendship with Joanne; the other was whether he would be fit enough to ride in Monday's races. It was impossible to say which caused him the greater worry.

Three

Throughout the journey to the Skalbrooke motocross circuit on the Monday morning in their minivan Greg Shearsmith and his father had been totally absorbed by their conversation. They were discussing the finer points of the re-tuning that Mr Shearsmith had carried out on his son's machine, the ebony-coloured custom-built Shearsmith Special. It appeared that Harry Shearsmith had worked on it non-stop throughout the weekend to ensure that it would be in peak condition for the opening race: a race which Greg himself, predictably, expected to win by the length of a street.

Lee was quite content just to listen to them, though most of the time he was deep in his own thoughts. The Shearsmiths had greeted him cheerfully enough when picking him up at his home and Lee was assured that his own bike had been given 'the once-over' by 'the wizard with the spanners', as Greg sometimes called his father. Certainly the green-and-silver bike looked in prime condition, especially after Lee had cleaned some old mud from the nobbly tyres and added a little polish to the metalwork. Mechanically, his machine had never let him down once since Mr Shearsmith had taken charge of it. In spite of all the care he lavished on the Special, he always found time to try and improve the performance of Lee's conventional factory model.

Now, as the minivan turned on to the lane leading to the circuit and bounced over some deep and ancient ruts, Lee had to brace himself to counteract the effect of the jolts. But he was a split-second too late for the first and worst of them and he couldn't help grimacing with the pain.

'You all right, son?' was the anxious inquiry from Mr Shearsmith who, by chance, had been turning to face him at that moment. 'You look a bit pale, you know.'

'I'm O.K., thanks,' replied Lee, making a gallant attempt at a smile. 'Just caught off-balance.'

In fact, he was feeling far from fine. In spite of the strapping he'd contrived to put round his torso he still regularly experienced stabs of pain from the area of the rib-cage where Haylin's toe-cap had gone in. He kept telling himself that the pains weren't as sharp as they had been over the weekend – and that they wouldn't affect his capabilities in a fiercely competitive race. After all, every rider suffered some mishap or other that caused pain but he simply got on with

251

the business of riding as fast as he could go and so forgot about the aches. All the same, Lee admitted to himself, if to no one else, that he couldn't be sure he'd last out an entire race programme in his present state of health.

To his dismay, the first people he saw as he wheeled his bike down the ramp from the mini-van into the car park were Uncle Ken, Joanne and Darren. He'd hoped to avoid contact with any of them until he knew for certain how he would cope with the demands of racing. Luckily, Daz, as usual, didn't waste much time before going off on his own, leaving Uncle Ken to attend to the pre-race preparation of his bike. However, he didn't miss the opportunity to utter a typically uncomplimentary remark to his brother.

'Hey, you look as if you've just been two rounds with the world's worst boxer – and lost by a knock-out,' he guffawed. 'Well, see you later, kiddo – probably when I lap you in the first race!'

Daz disappeared towards the pits area without a backward glance or another word to his uncle. Doubtless, Lee decided, he was going to tell his cronies the hilarious story of how his kid brother had been beaten up by mistake – and then how he, Darren Parnaby, planned to win three races in a row to prove he was the undisputed champion of the Intermediates' class at Skalbrooke (or anywhere else he happened to favour with his membership).

252

Joanne, who had been paying close attention to a sparkling new Honda, now hurried across to have a word with Lee.

'Are you really all right, Lee?' she inquired anxiously. 'Daz was telling us how you'd been clobbered by a bunch of thugs – older boys. Said you'd hurt your ribs, or claimed you had. Daz thought it was an excuse in case you didn't win a race today – but then he would.'

'Of course I'm all right!' Lee snapped. He was thoroughly fed up with being fussed over by his mother and people like Mr Shearsmith. They seemed to think he was as fragile as an ice-cream cornet. Well, he wasn't. He was a lot tougher than Daz, for a start. 'I wouldn't be here if I wasn't fit to race.'

'Oh, good,' Joanne replied warmly, and beamed. 'Well – what do you think of the bike then? Don't you think she looks terrific?'

She turned towards the gleaming red racing-bike, holding out her arm, wrist cocked, as if about to introduce it to Lee like a person.

'Great,' said Lee coolly. 'But it's not the bike that counts. It's what the rider can do that really matters when the heat's on.'

'Oh yes, of course,' Joanne agreed. But her face had the look of someone who'd just been told her birthday-treat was cancelled.

'See you,' Lee muttered and hurried away.

He was well aware that he'd hurt her by his attitude

253

but he simply wasn't in the mood to chat about someone else's new bike and racing-prospects. His own worries were uppermost in his mind and he had a sinking feeling that his injury was going to hamper his chances in a race, perhaps severely. But he had to face that problem on his own.

Joanne's appearance had surprised him. Her auburn hair was normally shoulder-length but she'd had it cut shorter than many a boy's (though it hardly compared with Greg Shearsmith's style for he was practically a skinhead). It made her look quite different and he didn't know whether he liked the change. Still, it was nothing to do with him, he decided; his thoughts swiftly returned to the urgent topic of what might happen in the first race of the day.

'Hey, heard the great news?' Greg greeted him exultantly when they met near the starting line. 'Graham Relton's not racing. He's had to pull out on doctor's orders with a trapped nerve in his back. So now I won't have a rival in sight!'

'How did that happen?'

Greg shrugged. 'Constant jarring on the back muscles while riding, so his dad says. Supposed to be a built-in risk for motocrossers. But not if you're fit like me – oh, and you as well I suppose. Anyway, Lee, I reckon it'll just be you and me fighting out the lead – well, until I decide to go flat out and leave you way, way behind, mate!'

'No, you've got it wrong as usual, Greg. You mean,

me first, you *second*. Still, it's rotten luck on Graham. Sounds as if he could be out of action for a long spell.'

Instead of boosting Lee's confidence the news about Graham's injury actually reduced it, in spite of what he'd just told Greg. For it made him think of his own physical state and that nagging ache in his side. He couldn't help worrying about the effect on his body of the incessant pounding caused by the jumps that were so much a part of a motocross circuit. Moreover, there was always the risk of a spill as a result of someone else's carelessness or sheer bad luck.

'Snap out of it, Lee! Think positively!' he told himself fiercely as he warmed up the engine of his green-and-silver racing-bike. It always felt good to be back in action and edging towards the starting-tape. At the start of the season he'd adopted a fresh philosophy: that whatever went wrong he would forget it as soon as humanly possible. He'd always look forward, not back; his view would be of victory, never defeat. *That* was positive thinking.

With Graham Relton, hitherto undisputed leader among the Intermediates, now out of the reckoning, Lee mentally listed the other contenders for race honours apart from himself and Greg Shearsmith. There was bound to be a very strong challenge from Duncan McGlew, nicknamed 'The Flying Scot', who was now adapting brilliantly to motocross after some years spent riding on grass tracks. Then there was

255

Nathan Pike, with whom Lee had once run a dead-heat. Nat was a great believer in tactical riding, sometimes lying up with the leaders, at other times making a late strong run from the rear. Like Duncan, the quiet and determined Nat was a member of several clubs but nowadays he never missed a Skalbrooke meeting because, he claimed, it provided him with the highest-quality opposition.

Finally, of course, there was Darren who, at that very moment, thrust his front wheel into the tape in his impatience to get a flying start. It was the sort of offence Daz committed fairly frequently. This time the official starter, Mr Ottershaw, showed his irritation by the manner in which he ordered Daz to get back into line.

Lee, who'd been drawn near the middle of the line, toyed with the throttle as he tried to judge to perfection the moment when the starter would send the tape zinging sideways. Always, in every competitor, there was the strongest desire to make the fastest getaway. Lee had become adept at the art; and now he was praying that his skill had not deserted him on this vital occasion.

Yet it seemed he'd missed the break this time. The surge of riders on either side of him took Lee by surprise: and in his haste to join them he almost stalled his engine. Even so, he wasn't so far behind the leading bunch as he weaved to gain a good position for taking the first bend, a severe left-hander. Then, just as he was congratulating himself on making up lost ground, he glimpsed the fluttering red flag held high by an official on the edge of the track itself.

The race was being stopped, the riders being recalled, because of a false start.

The culprit, no one was surprised to learn, was Darren Parnaby who, once again, had charged the tape in an effort to be first away. Mr Ottershaw was no longer merely annoyed: he was furious. With everyone listening avidly, Daz received a public warning that if he repeated the offence once more he would be banned from the entire meeting, and probably from the next meeting as well. He was a persistent offender and he had to be taught a lesson. For this first race he was to be penalised by starting fifteen seconds behind everyone else.

Predictably, Darren tried to argue against that ruling but Mr Ottershaw simply finger-waved him into silence. Glumly, Daz backed his machine out of the line-up.

Lee was just putting his helmet on again when he heard a familiar voice saying to him: 'Dad said only yesterday that Daz was becoming too wild for his own good! He really will get suspended one of these days.' He hadn't realised that Joanne had been drawn so close to him in the start line. She was wearing a pale blue helmet and a typically wide grin. Clearly she didn't bear Lee any grudge for the curt way he'd

258

treated her earlier. Now he just nodded that he'd heard and thought how relaxed she appeared.

When the tape sprang apart a few seconds later Lee was instantly among the leaders. That initial bend had never caused him any real trouble and it didn't now as he skidded through it in tandem with Greg Shearsmith. Greg, inwardly rejoicing that two of his chief rivals, Graham Relton and Daz Parnaby, were effectively out of contention, was determined to make the most of his improved chances of winning. His first aim was to put young Lee in his place – which, at best, would be second.

The sheer power of the Shearsmith Special was seen to full effect in the next few hundred metres. Even before he reached the edge of the copse at the top of the long incline Greg had opened up an astonishing lead. Lee, his nearest pursuer, could scarcely believe the evidence of his eyes; how on earth had Greg got so far ahead? Clearly Harry Shearsmith's genius as a tuner was to the fore again – allied to his son's rocket-style of racing. Already some spectators were thinking that only a serious mistake on his part, or a mechanical failure, could prevent Greg from seizing a famous victory – and the first lap wasn't even half completed!

Just before they reached the trees Lee discovered he held second place only by the slenderest margin. Ranging alongside him was Nathan Pike. The identity of his challenger was another surprise for Lee:

259

normally Nat preferred to pounce from the rear in the final stages of a race. Now, however, he'd decided on fresh tactics. It was not only Greg's soaraway start but also the amount of dust on the track that had caused Nat to chase the leaders without delay.

Behind them the field was well strung-out. Duncan McGlew was a casualty at the first bend after colliding with an inexperienced rider who'd braked at the wrong moment. In untangling himself from his fallen rival and then retrieving his machine he had the assistance of a number of spectators and marshals – and between them they'd impeded Darren. So, to his ill-concealed fury, Daz lost further precious time in his efforts to catch up with everyone else.

Duncan and Darren exchanged mild insults before the young Scot with the carrot-coloured hair accelerated from the trouble spot to leave Daz fuming in his wake. The boy who'd been the cause of the trouble in the first place was helped from the scene by an unsympathetic father. Garry Talbot, whose own father was present to urge him on to show ambition and imagination, was among the stragglers again whereas Joanne had already made good progress into the middle of the group lying behind Lee and Nat.

The track narrowed and zig-zagged through the trees and was hardly the place for overtaking. Nonetheless, Nathan was pushing hard all the time to get past Lee and become the main challenger to Greg.

Lee instinctively clenched his teeth as he resisted his rival.

By the time they approached the bomb-hole, the most famous and feared obstacle on the course, Lee was leading by no more than the diameter of a wheel. The descent into the crater, however, held no terrors for him. He had taught himself to be at his best when riding downhill, even when the gradient, as here, was one-in-four. There was no way Nat Pike was going to emerge first over the far rim.

Yet the keenness to stay ahead proved to be his undoing. His momentum up the slope carried him to a tremendous height as he leapt over the edge: and so, inevitably, the landing was bone-shaking. The jab of pain in his ribs took his breath away and his control over the bike was lost, momentarily. The front wheel wavered as it touched the ground and it seemed to spectators (always in good numbers at that point) that the machine was going to heel over.

It was his instinct for self-preservation that saved Lee. Somehow he overcame the pain, changed gear and regained control. There was a thin cheer from the crowd: and some of the applause was also for Nathan Pike. For the quietly-spoken rider from Rockleigh rarely missed an opening – and he hadn't missed the one presented by Lee's misfortune. Touching down perfectly from his leap from the crater, he shot past his wavering rival into second place. On his tail was a competitor riding as he'd never ridden before and

thus the pair of them pushed Lee down into fourth place.

Meanwhile, Greg Shearsmith was in the process of setting a remarkable lap-record. His positioning for every twist in the circuit was hardly less than perfect, his speed as he swept through a variety of obstacles quite astonishing. By the time he completed the first circuit he knew he was riding the race of his life. And he was exulting in the experience.

All that was to change completely soon after the start of the third lap.

Darren had been having a thoroughly frustrating time trying to overtake the sluggards at the rear of the field. Several were cluttering up the course and it required immaculate timing and bullying tactics to get past them. In spite of his determination to combine those needs Daz wasn't making the best progress. If he didn't break through in the next minute or so then, as he realised only too well, his chance of finishing among the leaders would be hopeless. Then, to his vast dismay, he discovered that Greg Shearsmith was about to pass *him*: he was in danger of being lapped.

That was a humiliation to be avoided at all costs. He knew who was attempting to thrust ahead of him – and he and Greg were deadly rivals. Greg thought he had chosen well the point where he wanted to overtake for it was just before the track narrowed ahead of the copse. Cleverly he gave the impression he was

263

going to take his rival on the outside: and then he switched inside with a burst of power. Daz, though, wasn't to be tricked that way. As Greg drew alongside Daz recklessly leaned in on him.

There was no way that Greg could avoid the contact. Inevitably, he lost balance – and, because legs and bikes had tangled, Daz was pulled remorselessly over with him. Both riders crashed through the tapes marking the track; and a tail-ender they'd both just overtaken wasn't able to prevent himself from cannoning into them.

Daz, because he'd fallen uppermost, was the first to get to his feet. And, in his fury at what had occurred, he swung a punch at Greg.

Four

The blow caught Greg on the shoulder just as he was about to rise. But it was his own surprise, rather than the force of it, that sent him flat on his back again. Greg, who wasn't unfamiliar with rough-house tactics, didn't try to stand up again immediately: instead he reached out for Darren's ankle and succeeded in jerking him off his feet. As Daz hit the ground Greg, getting to his knees, let go with his first retaliatory punch.

The tubby tail-ender, who had been brought down but not hurt, was Garry Talbot and he stood and watched in amazement as the combatants grappled with each other. But he stood in the middle of the track as if guarding his machine, its front wheel still spinning, and was oblivious of the approach of Nat Pike and Lee Parnaby, who'd just regained third place in the race. The nearest marshal was racing towards the scene from the edge of the copse as Nat, unable to get past the heap of bikes on the track, skidded almost broadside into them and thus joined the former race leader on the ground.

Lee very nearly got through the pile-up. He actually rode right over Garry's rear-wheel and saddle before he was brought to earth by colliding with the fork of his brother's machine. Luckily, he didn't suffer any further damage in the fall but again there were twinges of protest from the ribs region. That merely added to his anger at being put out of the race in such dreadful circumstances. For he'd seen at once that it was Daz, ever recognisable in his yellow-and-black helmet, who was trading punches with Greg.

By now, the clash between Greg and Darren had moved up a gear. Greg, having landed a couple of really hefty blows, was prepared to call it off and get back into the race, even though he couldn't hope to win now. But Daz, enraged by a blow on the ear, unprotected since his helmet had fallen off, wasn't giving up until he had flattened his opponent.

The marshal was uncertain what to do: he could hold up a flag to stop the race because of a pile-up, then try to separate the battling boys or summon help from officialdom. He dithered and as he did so more riders came to a full stop or tried to continue via illegal routes. At last an official arrived and, seeing how bad matters were, used his walkie-talkie to ask Mr Cantrill, the secretary, to come over immediately. Then, after ordering the marshal to display a red flag to halt the race, he took positive action to break up the fight.

266

Two seconds earlier, however, Lee had made his own move. 'Cut it out, you stupid fools!' he yelled, and launched himself bodily into the fray. It was a good thing he was wearing so much protective clothing because otherwise the swinging punch he took from Daz would have laid him out. As it was, the force of Darren's gloved fist landing on the side of his helmet sent Lee sprawling into a stationary Suzuki straddled by a flabbergasted spectator. Lee hadn't even seen the blow coming but he was to feel the effects of it for a long time. Initially, it made him feel sick and dizzy and he was glad of the help of the person who removed his helmet for him.

Greg had dropped his fists on seeing what had happened to Lee but, after a cursory glance at his victim, Daz was about to launch another assault on Greg when, at last, the official managed to get between them and stop the conflict.

'How're you feeling now, Lee?' someone asked anxiously; and Lee, opening his eyes again, found Joanne kneeling beside him.

'O.K. Just a bit of a headache,' he mumbled, though that wasn't the truth. The queasiness hadn't gone yet and the pain was back in his side. But the worst feeling was one of acute embarrassment. Once again he'd been hurt physically and dumped on the ground without his being able to defend himself. He'd been made to look like a weakling anyone could crush with ease.

'I told you Dad said Darren had become a bit wild –
well, I reckon this proves it,' Joanne continued.

Peter Cantrill, Skalbrooke's discipline-minded
secretary, appeared to think so, too. After questioning the marshal and asking some bystanders about the
sequence of events leading to the exchange of blows
he delivered to Daz and Greg a strong condemnation
of their conduct which, he said, was disgraceful.

'Absolutely disgraceful,' he thundered in case no
one had heard the word the first time. 'That members
of this club should *fight* with each other, in public,
what's more, is something utterly beyond my understanding. But then, you two have been in trouble
before, haven't you? There was that time when I
found you, Gregory, engaged in illegal practising at
the Autodrome. And you, Darren, have been giving
trouble to the Starter on several occasions, with the
result that you were officially penalised for this very
race.'

He paused at that point but it was for effect rather
than to give anyone the opportunity of making a
comment. Daz and Greg, who'd been glowering at
each other before Mr Cantrill started to speak, were
now looking distinctly worried. They sensed that
they were going to be punished severely.

'As you have caused a great deal of trouble to
everyone by bringing this race to a premature finish
through your total selfishness,' the secretary
resumed. 'I must take steps to see that such a thing
268

cannot happen again, at least for the next few races in your category. Accordingly, you will not be permitted to ride again today or at the next meeting, a fortnight hence. If there is any repetition of your misbehaviour after that your membership of the Skalbrooke Club will be withdrawn forthwith. Do you understand, both of you?'

For some moments neither Daz nor Greg was able to speak or make any movement. The sentence was little short of death to their ambitions: far worse than they could have imagined. But they knew from club

rules that there was no appeal against it. The secretary's judgment was law. They nodded jerkily and began to wonder how they could possibly survive without the high excitement of circuit competition.

Mr Cantrill hadn't finished with his strictures. Apart from the shameful conduct of Gregory and Darren, he said, most other riders had been at fault in going far too fast without regard for the safety of themselves or fellow-competitors. There seemed to have been a collective madness, as he put it, about the entire race (which was a bit unfair on Garry Talbot, for one, but it didn't occur to him to object to being called a madman). In such lightning fast conditions on the track responsible riders took extra, not less, care. Let this be a warning to all.

'Right,' he concluded with the thinnest of smiles that made him begin to look human again. 'This race is hereby abandoned. The Seniors' race will start in five minutes. So I suggest you Intermediates use this interval to think sensibly about your tactics for your next race.'

'That's diabolical!' Daz exploded the moment he was sure Mr Cantrill was out of earshot. All traces of enmity having drained away in the common disaster, he stared at Greg and beseeched him: 'What are we going to do now?'

Greg grinned and gave a shrug. He was rarely down for long. 'Don't worry, Daz. We'll think of something. Now I'd better see if the Special's all right.'

While he and his father, who'd been a silent spectator during the secretary's speeches, went into a huddle over their precious bike Daz at last spared his brother a glance.

'Feeling better now?' he inquired, though with no hint in his tone that he was remotely interested in the answer.

'Terrific, actually,' was Lee's sarcastic reply. 'No thanks to you, though.'

'Well, I told you before, little brother: you shouldn't get yourself involved in things that have nothing to do with you.' He paused and then added as an afterthought: 'Especially when you haven't a clue how to defend yourself. No-wonder you finish up on the deck so often.'

Before Lee could think of a suitable rejoinder Daz went across to his bike, gave it a perfunctory inspection and then wheeled it away from the track. He expected his uncle to carry out a proper examination when he got it back to the pit area.

'Are you really O.K., Lee?' his cousin was asking anxiously. 'Honestly, you still look a bit dazed to me. Daz really is a heartless lout at times, isn't he? After all, you were trying to save *him* from more trouble. . . .'

'I don't think I'll bother to race again today,' Lee announced. 'It's nothing to do with that knock I got from Daz. That accident I had the other day – I don't think the damage has quite healed – probably shook it

271

up a bit on some of the jumps today.'

'That's a rotten shame,' Jo told him with total
sympathy. 'The next race won't be the same without
you in it. You know, I was really hoping to catch you
up last time. Honestly, I wasn't all that far behind. I
was enjoying myself even more than I thought I
would. You must feel really sick at having to give up
today.'

However, when he made his way home that afternoon it wasn't the loss of his racing that Lee was
thinking about. He was remembering Darren's
remark about his inability to defend himself when
under attack.

Five

'*Key-AI*!' Lee yelled in unison with everyone else, at the same time advancing smartly, his arms moving like pistons, his clenched fists twisting on imaginary impact in the manner of drills biting into a tough surface.

The instructor nodded his approval and ordered: 'Again.'

This time he found fault with the way in which Lee was transferring his weight from his back foot to his front foot. 'Smoother – give it more thrust. Good, that's it!'

Lee relished the praise. After all, it was obvious that Rick, the Karate instructor, was a perfectionist. If he said that a student was doing well, then that student was doing very, very well. Now it was Lee's ambition to be the best student Rick had ever taught.

Yet, the previous week, when he'd attended a class for the first time, he wasn't at all sure he was going to like it or get anything out of it. He'd noticed in the

273

local weekly paper an advertisement for weekly karate classes for beginners to be held in the Village Institute. It was the headline that caught his eye: 'Defend yourself – against ANYONE'. That might, he felt, have been written just for him. However, he was easily the youngest person to join the class and it seemed to him that the instructor devoted most of his time to the older people. In any case, they appeared to enjoy the courteous and rather formal manner in which the students were supposed to treat each other. They kept bowing to one another and murmuring polite expressions. Lee thought much more aggression was needed all round.

His view changed, however, when shouting was introduced. The favoured word was *kai*, which sounded like 'key-ai.' It was intended, Rick explained, to act as an encouragement or a spur to purposeful, forward moves. At the same time, the explosive way in which it was uttered actually helped one's breathing. Lee immediately decided he thoroughly approved of that expression. He tended to shout it anywhere when he was sure he wasn't going to be overheard. Certainly its use spurred him on to practise his new stances and movements whenever he had a few minutes to spare. He'd even taken to trying them out in front of a long mirror, a training tip passed on by Rick at the conclusion of the first lesson.

So far he'd managed to keep his riveting new interest a secret from everyone: well, everyone who

274

mattered. Daz would be scornful, his mother worried and Greg simply wouldn't understand, thinking the whole procedure pointless and quite unnecessary. But then, Greg was older and heavier than Lee: and he *looked* tough, if only because of his hairstyle, or lack of it. Lee took care of his own helmet of fair hair, which was on the long side, as his mother kept reminding him. He certainly didn't want Andy Haylin and his thugs to know what he was up to; if ever they turned on him again he wanted to surprise them. They wouldn't know what he was capable of and then he'd really get his own back for what he'd suffered.

'Right,' Rick called from the centre of the hall. 'Let's all split up into pairs. Pick somebody as near your own height and weight as possible. We're going to practise some blocking movements. Come on then, move smartly.'

The only person among the score of students who matched Lee's requirements was a girl called Sharon. She was at least a year older and, so she'd already told him, much more experienced because she'd attended a night class in karate a couple of years earlier. Lee would have preferred to practise with someone else but he knew that when he became an expert he'd be able to take on *anybody*, whether older or much heavier and taller. For the present, he must simply take every opportunity to learn whatever he could from anyone more knowledgeable than himself.

Just before they started on the prime defence techniques each pair was shown how to swing the body smoothly, pivoting from the hips. Balance, they were told for the umpteenth time, was of paramount importance.

When it was his turn to demonstrate the blocking movements with his forearms Lee believed he knew exactly what to do because he'd practised them the previous week. Sharon, however, was keen to prove how fast and accurate she was as an attacker. Her right fist snaked in, aiming for his solar plexus as she'd been taught, and when Lee managed to twist his body fractionally the blow caught him in the ribs.

For a second he was angry with himself for being so slow in his defence; but then he realised that although he'd certainly felt the blow there was no residue of pain, so his old injury from the Haylin attack seemed to have cleared up.

To her surprise, he grinned happily at Sharon and then employed the perfect scything motion with the hard edge of his palms to frustrate her next assault. She winced as the blows cut into her arms.

'You're learning fast, you are,' she told him ruefully.

'That's the idea,' he told her chirpily, and then blocked successfully as she launched another sharp attack, aiming this time for the vulnerable neck area.

When they switched roles, however, Sharon's defence was practically impregnable. But then, as she

276

admitted, it was her speciality. It was obvious she was very pleased to have kept Lee's concentrated attacks at bay.

'O.K. everyone!' Rick yelled loudly to bring all activity to a halt. 'It's nearly time to finish but I want to tell you I've seen good progress being made. But before you all think you're becoming experts let me also tell you that the Japanese, who invented karate, would spend a month – yes, a whole *month* – mastering just one of those blocking movements. That's right, one single movement. And that's not on a weekly basis – they'd practise every spare minute, every day of the week. *That's* dedication, for you.'

The instructor paused a moment for that humbling piece of information to sink in; then, he added, the session would end with an opportunity to practise what he called 'the low level swoop'. But first, a demonstration. . . .

When, a couple of minutes later, Lee launched his first swoop on Sharon he met with immediate, and immensely satisfying, success. The trick was to duck low when being attacked, grab your opponent's front knee and ankle, simultaneously pushing in opposite directions; the victim, unable to remain on his feet, falls. But, holding on to his leg so that he can't scramble free, you then deliver a 'killer' punch to the unprotected groin, stomach or chin. As the instructor had pointed out, 'If that doesn't finish the argument then you should never have taken up karate in the

first place. It's not a game for the squeamish, you know.'

Sharon went down with an ominous thump and then Lee only just managed to pull the punch that was intended for the pit of the stomach. Gallantly he helped her up but in the process he stepped heavily on her toes. As karate is practised in bare feet she wasn't really hurt but she hopped around for effect. After that, she decided she'd had enough for one week. Lee, however, couldn't help feeling that he'd learned a lot already.

Before they went over to the drinks of orange that

had been laid out for everybody, the pairs bowed formally to each other and murmured what sounded like '*uss*', which Lee understood to mean 'O.K., thanks.' The style of the whole thing wasn't so bad after all, he decided.

'What made you take this up?' Sharon asked him unexpectedly.

'Oh, er, I, er – I was a bit bored at home,' Lee muttered unconvincingly, unwilling to disclose the real reason.

'You were probably being bashed up by bigger boys – that's the usual reason kids decide to learn how to defend themselves,' Sharon remarked with surprising and devastating accuracy. 'Well, the way you're shaping up, they're in for a shock next time they pick on you. But keep it up, Lee. Make yourself as tough as possible. You have to be really hard if you want to stay on top.'

He looked at her with new interest. She'd summed him up brilliantly, he felt. Once he was set on a course of action he rarely allowed anything to deflect him from it.

'What about you?' he asked, not only out of politeness.

'My reason had nothing to do with bullying – well, not the usual kind, anyway. My dad owns the new leisure centre and he wants his kids to be top in everything. But I wasn't going to have him watching me all the time like a hawk whenever I was trying to learn something. I like to do things in my own way, in my own time. Dad hasn't a clue what goes on in this place, so that's why I signed on here. One day I'll give him a real knock-out of a surprise.'

Cog-wheels were meshing in Lee's brain.

'Is your name Talbot, then?'

'Yes. My dad's Ted Talbot. Why, have you –'

'– so you have a brother called Garry? Who's just started riding in motocross?'

'Yes, but he won't be much good. He's no good at anything, really. Partly that's because Dad pushes him so hard. But, really, Garry's just not interested.

He likes a lazy life. Fishing's the only thing he's any good at and that's not a proper sport, is it? Anyway, how do you know him?'

Lee hesitated only fractionally before deciding to tell her the story of how he'd been beaten up in mistake for Darren by thugs allegedly looking after the interests of her brother. He was beginning to take to this girl with shrewd grey eyes and wavy blonde hair and an uncomplicated manner.

'Oh, them – Haylin and his mates,' she said contemptuously. 'That's typical of their thinking. They're trying to get in with Dad – well, Haylin is. Wants Dad to put on a wrestling match so that Haylin's father can take part. No chance, I reckon, but Haylin doesn't know that. But it's why he's sucking up to Dad and trying to get in with Garry and me. I just told him I didn't want to know him, full stop. But he daren't risk upsetting me in case I finish his chances with Dad.'

Lee didn't know whether to be thankful for this news or angry. Plainly Haylin and his hangers-on were unlikely to bother him or Darren again if they were merely trying to curry favour with Garry and not acting as his official protectors. On the other hand, if what Sharon said was true, then he had suffered injury and humiliation for no reason at all. Haylin had simply carried out the attack on a whim. Even so, that still didn't improve his feelings about Darren.

'You look a bit sick, Lee,' said Sharon, breaking

into his thoughts. 'Isn't the juice agreeing with you or something?'

'Er, no, it's O.K. Look, I think I'd better get out of this gear and get off. Can't stay here all day.'

'Well, if it doesn't take you an age to change I'll walk up the road with you. I've got a bit of time to kill before my bus comes.'

Lee didn't know how to cope with that suggestion so he muttered something that might have been anything and darted away to the changing-rooms. Then he realised that might be interpreted as eagerness not to keep her waiting. Slowly he took off the loose white tunic (or *gi* as it was known) that was always worn for karate: and was slower still in folding it carefully into the old rucksack he'd borrowed from his father's kit. He'd bought the tunic, secretively, entirely with his own money and the last thing he wanted was for Darren to discover it. At home he hid it behind the spare blankets at the top of the airing-cupboard.

He lingered over dressing and, especially, combing his hair, checking his watch every thirty seconds. By now, he decided eventually, she'd have got fed up waiting for him and gone off on her own.

She hadn't.

'Hi,' she greeted him cheerfully as they simultaneously emerged from the side-by-side changing rooms. 'That's good timing.'

As they walked along the street Lee could only keep his fingers crossed that no one he knew was observing them. Sharon, however, was displaying great interest in his motocross activities. She appeared to think it was a sport she herself would enjoy; and, as she pointed out, she couldn't be worse at it than her feeble brother. Lee, feeling cheered again, appreciated that point of view.

'Well, see you at karate next week, Lee,' she said as her bus rolled to a stop. 'If you get into any fights before then, I don't think you'll be the loser.'

Lee sprinted towards home and hoped she was right.

Six

Lee was furious at being forced to change his plans. He slammed shut the kitchen door and ignored his mother's threat: 'You can cut that out or I'll stop your pocket money!' Upstairs, he flung open the bedroom door with such force that it bounced on its hinges. Even Darren looked alarmed by this tempestuous display.

Still unable to calm down, he jerked a shirt from his drawer and then felt a pinch of satisfaction as he tugged a button off. Even if his mother noticed its absence there wouldn't be time for it to be replaced before they all left for the hospital. After all, he shouldn't have been wearing a freshly washed best shirt: he should be decked out in leathers, elbow protectors, smooth-soled boots and helmet. Instead of getting ready to visit a relative in hospital he should have been preparing for the first race of the day on his beloved green-and-silver motorbike.

'I shouldn't have to go to see Aunt Sue,' he com-

284

plained. 'You're the one Uncle Ken fusses over. It's *your* bike he looks after, not mine. So you should be going to see her, not me.'

'I am going,' Daz replied mildly.

'I mean on your own,' Lee amended. 'They don't need me.'

'In this family loyalty is supposed to be important, little brother,' Daz said piously. 'So you've got to be kind to dear Aunt Sue and tell her you hope she's feeling better after her emergency operation. I don't see why that's so hard for you to do.'

'Because I should be racing this afternoon, that's why,' was the savage rejoinder. 'You're banned from racing so this meeting doesn't matter to you. You've got nothing else to do but visit *your* favourite aunt in hospital.'

Daz, who didn't seem to want to get immersed in an argument, just shrugged and attended to the knot in his vivacious tie. Both boys had been ordered by their mother to look their best: nothing less than jackets, ties and clean shirts would do. Lee had tried to point out that it didn't matter one scrap what *they* looked like: surely the important factor was how Aunt Sue looked. Mrs Parnaby insisted that hospital patients didn't want visitors who resembled tramps. Lee's final plea to be allowed to go straight from the hospital to the motocross had also been rejected out of hand: that was when he stormed out of the kitchen.

As he slumped into the back seat of the car for the

285

drive to Skalbrooke General Hospital Lee unkindly hoped that the old Ford would break down before they were clear of the village. If they had no option but to return home. . . .

Daz, who naturally enough was sitting up front, entered into a spirited conversation with his mother. They speculated on where his father might be at that moment: ultimately they decided he'd be ashore in Australia, trying to take unusual pictures of kangaroos. Photography was his latest hobby and when his ship was in port he posted off to them what he described as 'rushes' of his most recent snaps. He seemed to have a passion for shots of exuberant animals, probably, as Darren remarked, because he didn't see much wild life at sea, if one discounted sharks and under-nourished seagulls.

'You haven't got much to say for yourself, Lee,' his mother remarked, turning to glance into the back. 'If you're sulking, you can stop it this minute.'

'Well, you two seem to be getting on well enough without me,' Lee pointed out reasonably enough.

'Listen, you'd better find something to say to Joanne when we get to the hospital. You've been neglecting her completely of late. Remember, you're very much in her debt when you think of all Ken and Sue have done for you and your precious motor-cycling.'

'Oh, he'll find something to say to *Joanne* because she's a girl,' Darren put in with the smile of the innocent. 'He likes talking to *girls*. He was out with a new one the other day. A blonde, a bit older than him, I believe. Well, poor Joanne's going to be really jealous when she hears about it.'

Initially, Lee was astonished. Daz hadn't said a thing about this to *him*. It was so unlike him not to taunt Lee whenever he came into possession of information that Lee would rather keep secret. Then he began to seethe. It really was typical of Daz to try to create trouble in the slyest way possible.

Mrs Parnaby had another quick, and very interested, look over her shoulder.

'Is this true, Lee?'

'He's talking rubbish as usual, utter rubbish,' Lee retaliated, careful not to make a complete denial. 'I don't go out with blondes or girls of any other colour. Darren's covering up for something he doesn't want you to know about. That's one of his favourite tactics. You should know that, Mum.'

Lee knew that was a feeble counter-attack but he couldn't think of anything else to say. His mind was on Sharon, wondering whether it was Daz himself who'd seen them together. Nothing, though, would induce him to ask that question.

Having scored that underhand success, Darren didn't speak again until they reached the hospital; and, thankfully, Mrs Parnaby didn't pursue the matter of her younger son's alleged girl friend. Lee, sprawling all over the back seat as an act of dumb defiance, was *willing* Daz to say something really provocative when they were next alone together. This time he wouldn't hesitate. He'd jump on his brother and demonstrate just what he'd learned at karate. The thought of what he would do to Daz gave Lee immense satisfaction. Really, it was inevitable that Daz would commit some offence that screamed out to be punished.

Skalbrooke General gave the impression that it was the most popular spot to visit in the entire county. Even after two tours of the twin car parks it was impossible to find a free space. Mrs Parnaby irritatedly rejected all Daz's recommendations to leave the car at points where 'Strictly No Parking' signs were prominent.

'Right then,' said Darren animatedly. 'This is a clear sign to us not to stay. Let's get off home again. At least we can say we *tried* to visit Aunt Sue. Anyway, I *hate* going into smelly, blood-stained hospitals ...'

'You amaze me, Daz,' Lee cut in. 'I thought all sadists like you *enjoyed* seeing other people suffer.'

Just as Mrs Parnaby was about to admonish him for that remark a Triumph reversed out of a parking bay in front of her to leave the space they'd been looking for; and in the manoeuvering that followed, Lee's comment was forgotten. Still, she remembered to warn them, as they entered the building, that there was to be no bickering in front of Aunt Sue. Neither boy bothered to reply to that.

Ward F was not hard to locate but Aunt Sue was not visible from the doorway because the long narrow room was as crowded as the car park. It was Lee who was the first to spot Joanne, sitting at her mother's bedside, apparently reading a letter to her.

Sue Wragby had a drip attached to one arm and looked as pale as the sheet covering her. The arrival of three more visitors seemed to cheer her up and she told Lee where extra seats could be found so that they could all sit comfortably around her bed. No one discussed any details of her operation but Mrs Parnaby told her sister-in-law, quite untruthfully, that she was looking well. Lee at that point was exchanging glances with Joanne. It didn't seem appropriate to him to talk about motocross but he couldn't think of anything else to mention. In any case, it wouldn't have been easy to hold a whispered conversation: the volume of noise was astonishing in a place where people were supposed to be ill.

The ward sister thought so, too. She moved round very purposefully, pointing out that the maximum number of visitors per bed was three. Mrs Parnaby protested that they'd only just arrived, which wasn't quite true, but she was politely told there could be no exceptions. For a moment or two, there was confusion and indecision. Then, simultaneously, Lee and Darren jumped to their feet.

By a margin so close it could hardly be measured, Darren was the first to declare his intentions.

'Look, you don't need me – I'll go now. Cheers everybody!'

'But it's not fair' – Lee was saying when his mother cut him off.

'Sit down, Lee! You're staying.'

'But it's just not *fair*!' he protested again, furious at the way he was being treated.

'What's fair has got nothing to do with it – and stop making a fuss,' Mrs Parnaby ordered. 'I dread to think what people will be saying about this family – quarrelling in a hospital ward.'

Lee dropped into his hard chair with a noise that brought another glare from his mother. He no longer cared what she said or what might happen to him. His day was utterly ruined. Then, to his astonishment, he saw that his brother had returned and was about to make an announcement.

'Forgot to tell you, Lee,' his brother said hurriedly, trying, but failing, to look genuinely apologetic. 'But there was a phone call for you just before we left home. From your mate Greg Shearsmith. Said would you ring him back when you had a moment. Said it was a bit urgent – the news he's got for you, I mean.'

He paused, smiled widely and added: 'Message delivered, then. Cheers again!'

'Hang on!' Lee yelled. But it was too late. Darren

was already through the door and away.

'He deliberately kept that phone call from me – that's typical of his rotten tricks,' Lee exploded.

'I've told you once, Lee, and I'll not tell you again: you'll sit there and you'll keep quiet,' his mother said, the hard edge of an ice axe in her voice. 'And don't you dare ask if you can go and make a phone call now. Don't you *dare*!'

So Lee sat there in dumb fury, avoiding even Joanne's sympathetic glances. He couldn't remember any time in his life when he'd felt so murderous about anyone. One day, though, he'd get his revenge on Darren. That revenge, he vowed, would be as sweet and long-lasting as he could make it.

Eventually visiting-time at Skalbrooke General ended. Aunt Sue looked as though the company of her family had revived her a little, in spite of the tensions that had been in evidence. Lee managed to force himself to give her a farewell kiss without being told to: but that kindly gesture didn't earn him a reprieve from his mother's condemnation. As they left the building she refused him permission to make a quick call from one of the public telephones that ranged along the wall near the Enquiry Office. He thought of saying that he needed to go to the Gents', adding that he'd catch them up in the car park. His mother, however, would see that as a not very subtle move and simply wait outside the door to the toilets until he emerged.

There was no sign of Darren when they reached the car but Mrs Parnaby expressed no surprise. Nor was she inclined to wait for him.

'He'll turn up at home when he's ready – and when he's hungry,' she commented as she put the car into reverse.

'But you should be mad with him for walking out on us like that,' Lee pointed out. 'You're just letting him get away with it.'

'Nonsense!' she declared. 'Compared to yours, his conduct has been *perfect*. I just wish you had shown a tenth of the consideration for others that Darren showed this afternoon.'

292

That, as far as Lee was concerned, was the final blow.

It was mid-evening before Lee was able to get to a public, and therefore private, telephone and by then it seemed that his luck had turned at last. For it was Greg himself who answered and he couldn't keep the joyousness of his news out of his voice.

'Hey, it's terrific! I've been invited to compete at the Open Meeting at Linkland Cove Motocross Club – you know, that place on the south coast. Great circuit – one of the best in the country. My dad's got a mate down there – well, he's got mates in the trade everywhere – and he fixed it up for us. Oh, yeah – you're invited as well. Won't cost you a cent, Lee. Dad's mate, Kel Gibson, he's got a caravan down there, huge four-berther, and we can stay in that free of charge. Fantastic, don't you reckon? Oh, by the way, it's the weekend after next. We leave Friday tea-time.'

'Fantastic!' Lee fervently agreed.

At least, it would be if there were no objection at home to his making the trip: if he could persuade his mother that his behaviour away from home in the company of friends would be impeccable so that she wouldn't have to worry about him for a single minute. That, he was well aware, was not going to be easy in the present climate in the Parnaby household.

'Dad's already hard at work, giving the Special the

top treatment – then he'll have a go at yours as well, Lee,' Greg raced on. 'I reckon there'll be nobody to touch us on that track. We'll soak up the prizes and we'll soak up the sun. Can't be bad! Look, I'll give you a ring when I've got more details from Kel Gibson. O.K.?'

'Great,' murmured Lee, and left it at that. He didn't want to say anything to suggest he couldn't guarantee acceptance of the invitation. If he suspected that Lee might pull out, Greg was quite capable of offering the vacant place to someone else who would snap it up instantly.

Patiently, but with no little difficulty, Lee waited more than an entire day before he broached the matter with his mother. Her response was a total surprise to him.

'Yes, on one condition: that Darren is invited as well.'

'But –'

'No "buts," Lee! All you motor-cyclists are supposed to stick together in everything. It would be completely unfair for one of you to go on an outing of that nature, leaving the other one at home. That's not how families should exist: not in my eyes, anyway. If one's left behind then it'll cause all sorts of resentment and jealousies. I'm not tolerating that. So, if you want to go and enjoy yourself at Linkland Cove then Darren must go with you.'

Seven

The top loop of the circuit seemed to have been placed at the edge of the sky. After emerging, in a fairly gentle spiral, from a dell with turf like a trampoline, it rose steeply up the slope on the landward side of the headland. From virtually any point on that sharply-angled ascent the view was spectacular: for every rider appeared to be shooting to the sun.

Far to the left, the cliff fell away in a series of ledges that reached all the way down to the shore, mostly a broad expanse of sand around the headland and in the bay itself. The adverse effect of the camber at the summit of the loop kept all but the most reckless of riders in check; as an additional safety measure, however, there was a barrier of fairly solid rubber tyres previously used by industrial vehicles, plainly of gigantic dimensions. In every way, the Linkland Cove Motocross Club's circuit was a true test of nerve and balance and ambition.

'I can't wait to get going on this roller-coaster,'

announced Greg, literally rubbing his hands in anticipation of the delights in store. 'I'm going to have the ride of my life, no danger. They'll all have to watch out for the Shearsmith Special, ridden by the star guest from Skalbrooke.'

'Thanks very much – nice to know I'm not being overlooked,' Lee commented sarcastically. 'Personally, as long as I finish a mile ahead of Darren I won't care what else happens.'

On Harry Shearsmith's advice, Greg and Lee were exploring the circuit on foot before trying it out on wheels. By the time they'd reached Linkland Cove the previous evening after the long journey from Skalbrooke it was too dark to do more than have a casual look at the landscape. In any case, after locating the caravan and unloading all their belongings from the converted minibus that Mr Shearsmith employed as a transporter, the first requirement had been a meal. Rather than risk culinary disaster with unfamiliar cooking equipment in the caravan itself, Mr Shearsmith had taken them all into the fishing-village-cum-holiday-resort of the Cove itself in search of 'something really tasty'. They'd found that in the round shape of excellent and enormous pizzas followed by chocolate-coated Italian ice-cream. After that feast, everyone was ready only for bed.

That morning, Darren, determined to please, had risen first, collected milk from a nearby farm and a supply of water, cooked breakfast for everyone, washed up and folded all the bedding away. As if that wasn't enough, he then assisted Mr Shearsmith in routine maintenance tasks on all three bikes, something he rarely offered to do at home where Uncle Ken would have been glad of a helping hand. Even so, Lee wasn't impressed. He couldn't forgive Daz for coming on the trip in the first place. The Shearsmiths were his friends, not his brother's, and Daz should have had the decency to decline the invitation Harry Shearsmith had been forced to extend to him after Mrs Parnaby's ultimatum. Daz, understandably perhaps, hadn't seen it like that. This was a glittering opportunity to race again and so he'd seized it with both hands. What's more, he claimed his presence was needed to prove that Skalbrooke possessed a motocrosser of the highest class. Himself, of course.

In fact, the three boys who were staying in Kel Gibson's caravan in the permanent park on the other side of the headland were not the only riders from the Skalbrooke Club. By coincidence, Nathan Pike and his family were holidaying in the area and so Nat, who'd raced over the circuit on a previous visit, was going to be among the competitors. Greg and Lee had already met him when they called at the secretary's office; and Nat had given them a graphic account of the track's delights and defects, as he described them. But nothing Nat said had prepared Lee for his first view of that breathtaking route to the top of the loop.

'You know, I could really fancy a swim today,' Lee

remarked as he stood on the edge of the cliff and gazed at the distant sea. 'Funny really, because normally I don't care for messing about in water.'

It was not only the sight of those gentle waves that had stirred such thoughts. Already it was hot enough for many people to be lying around, sunbathing; Lee, in T-shirt and jeans, felt distinctly over-dressed. In the pits most of the mechanics were bare-chested while one of the competitors, a boy called Adrian Linthwaite, was strutting around in nothing more than a pair of white gym shorts, proclaiming that's how he would ride if only the officials would let him. Such an attitude didn't surprise his fellow-members of the Linkland Club for Adrian was the self-styled King of the Mountain Motocross. Not many were prepared to challenge that title. Adrian's reputation was well-earned: apart from his string of victories, he scarcely ever came off his bike. Whatever the hazards, he stuck to his machine like superglue.

'Swimming's for those who've got nothing exciting to do,' Greg told Lee as they made their way back to the pits. 'Go and have a dip when you've earned it by finishing second in a race – second to me, of course!'

When they rejoined Harry Shearsmith they found, much to their amazement, that Darren was still acting as his assistant by diligently checking on the cleanliness of the air-filters on all three bikes. He smiled a welcome at them but they weren't taken in by this hint that he'd reformed.

'So I'll know who to blame if anything goes wrong with my machine today,' Greg observed with a blank face. His father frowned but didn't say anything. He, too, was surprised by Daz's keenness to help and his general amiability.

'Oh, no, I don't want you to have any excuses like mechanical failure when I beat you out of sight,' Darren replied blandly. 'I want you to be in your very best form, Gregory. Same goes for little brother, too, of course.'

Greg, who detested his full name, scowled and then bent down to have a whispered conversation with his father. He had to put up with Daz's company for Lee's sake but he vowed that it wouldn't happen again. Now, though, his determination to finish ahead of Darren Parnaby rivalled Lee's.

All around them bikes were roaring into life, blue exhaust smoke was mushrooming skywards and riders were uniting, if only temporarily, with saddles. As ever, Lee thrilled to the sweet sound of his own engine and prayed that, this time, he was on the track to glory. His walk round the circuit had shown him where he should make his maximum thrust in each lap irrespective of his overall position in the race.

The draw had put him alongside Adrian Linthwaite who, after all, was attired in his usual racing outfit with the legend 'Linthwaite of Linkland l-e-a-d-s!' emblazoned across his chest. Just two places away on his other side in the line-up was Daz,

299

invariably eye-catching in his black-and-yellow striped helmet. Lee tried to forget about personalities. They came second to his own performance. If he rode at his best then he would finish in front of them all, he told himself. The jumps on this course, with the exception of the one at the climax of the loop, were really nothing out of the ordinary. But the switchback nature of the circuit demanded fine judgment of pace and perfect timing when attempting to overtake.

To his dismay, Lee failed to anticipate the moment when the tape snaked aside. Surprisingly, Adrian Linthwaite was not among the fastest starters, either. Side by side they raced for the first bend, a gentle right-hander, in the wake of probably a dozen riders. The leader, by a definable margin, was Greg Shearsmith. That was just where the Skalbrooke supporters who were present expected him to be and they raised a good cheer when Greg increased his advantage through a tricky zigzag section. After that he could really open up the throttle because the route through the dip between the headlands was comparatively straight. His spread of power and what it could do for a fearless competitor caused a few eyes to blink among the home supporters.

Daz, bumped by a novice in the middle of the zigzag, was still capable of forcing his way into third position behind another, but unidentified, visitor. Lee, jostling for supremacy in a private duel with

300

Adrian, was still in the middle of the pack by the time they reached the springboard to the notorious loop.

The first major casualty of the race occurred when the visiting rider holding second place was passed in the air by Daz Parnaby at the first jump after the dip. That experience so unnerved him that he landed askew, failed to straighten up and was then clipped by another bike as he fought to stay upright. The spill was still being cleared up as Lee and Adrian zoomed over the jump and then instinctively parted to avoid disaster. It was Lee who came out of that situation with an advantage; and, beginning to motor again at full chat, he went off in vengeful pursuit of Daz, now clear in second place.

At that point, Greg was already completing the loop. There was a scattering of applause from spectators as he soared up the straight, flicked through the gears to take the turn at the top and slid satisfyingly into exactly the right position for the bouncing descent. The whole sequence so delighted Greg that he decided, next time round, he would get a little closer to the safety barrier of tyres. That would give the crowd an extra thrill. Greg, as his Skalbrooke rivals knew, was always the showman. Ahead Greg could envisage only victory. Having negotiated the toughest part of the track with such aplomb, it was perfectly natural that he should be chock-full of confidence.

However, both the Parnaby brothers and Adrian Linthwaite were going equally well. Lee, in particular, found the ascent of the loop, and the swerve at the top, just as exhilarating an experience as Greg had. Used to the fast Skalbrooke circuits, he didn't slow as he made the turn – something which Adrian did automatically. But then, as it was becoming clear to the home supporters, Adrian normally didn't face the sort of frenzied opposition that Skalbrooke was providing on this occasion.

By the end of the first lap Greg was still comfortably ahead of the field, though he hadn't managed to extend his lead over Daz. Lee was closing on his brother – and Nathan was cutting the gap between Lee and himself. Nat, regarded by all who knew him as a model of patience, had decided that on such a circuit he couldn't afford to be too far behind at any stage. There were so few good opportunities for overtaking. In any case, he, too, was revelling in the challenges Linkland Cove kept presenting to the resourceful and unrelenting rider. In spite of the dry conditions and a lively sea breeze, very little dust was being thrown up for the surface of the track was in excellent condition.

Lee, having drawn away from Adrian, now had his sights firmly set on the wearer of the tiger-coloured helmet. He knew he had a new advantage over his brother: with no Uncle Ken present to send him tactical signals, Darren for once had to ride his own race. There was no one at all to tell him when to close up or when to block a rival. Daz had to make all his own decisions and he wasn't used to that. Still, as long as he didn't have any real crises to cope with the absence of his usual tutor and mechanic wouldn't matter. Lee, of course, had it in mind to provide his brother with one major problem that afternoon: how to deal with defeat. 'Little brother' clenched his teeth, did a brilliantly-controlled skid through the first of the spirals, headed for the loop again with the intention of improving his time on that section in every successive lap. Daz wouldn't be able to stand *that* sort of competition from anyone.

The home supporters were becoming increasingly worried by the failure of their own riders. Adrian Linthwaite was the only one in the first five: and even he was losing ground in fourth place as Nat Pike growled up on him. The Linkland Club was happy to entertain visitors but it seemed to many ambitious parents that hospitality was being taken too far in the Intermediates' event on the present evidence. Cries of encouragement were turning to roars of abuse, aimed entirely at their own competitors. 'Get stuck in, son!' was the very mildest of the advice being screamed at some strugglers in the middle of the pack. Even the occasional four-letter word was being used until other parents told the offenders to desist. Once before some members of the Linkland Club had been threatened with banishment from meetings if they persisted in such conduct. All the same, the pressure on the home riders to improve their positions was being increased all the time. One girl, whose mother had been tearing into her with the worst language of all, was so affected by the barrage of words that she made a total miscalculation on the next acute bend: trying, amazingly, to overtake on the outside, she merely succeeded in cannoning off her rival – that sent her off the track at right angles until she collided with a parked transporter. After being picked up by her disgusted parents, it was several minutes before she stopped trembling. For her it was definitely the last race of the day.

Luck was not on the side of the home team, either. Rupert Johnstone, Adrian's closest rival in club events, was desperately trying to get to the leaders when, cutting a corner, his chain got entangled with marker-tape. This threw the chain off, jamming it between swinging arm and sprocket. End of race for Rupert, too.

Meanwhile, Greg cruised serenely along, delighting himself and his father with his performance. The only danger to him was over-confidence, something that had been the cause of his downfall in the past. It was what his pursuers were hoping for: but Greg was in no mood to give anything away. His ban at Skalbrooke had hurt deeply, though he'd learned not to say too much in public about his emotions. The chance to ride over a new and thrilling track, one that undoubtedly suited his style of competition, was all he could have wished for: so he was making the most of his pleasure. From his ascendancy on the parallel parts of the track he could tell just how far ahead he was, even when Harry Shearsmith wasn't in a position to advise him. Greg was completely confident he could keep the Parnaby brothers at bay.

Lee was thinking more about overtaking Darren than anything else. Indeed, there *wasn't* anything else that mattered as much to him. Each lap his technique for tackling the loop improved fractionally: and so each lap he inched nearer to Darren's rear wheel. Behind Lee, Nathan was having a similar duel with Adrian; and it was beginning to look as though the visiting rider would soon be winning on points. Adrian, unused to being chivvied in this way, was beginning to feel irritated with himself as well as with his opponent. Instead of following his pre-determined line through the curves he tried to steer a shorter course. That wasn't wise. Twice, on bankings, he very nearly lost his balance and his bike, on the second occasion slewing right across the track before regaining direction and power – that was the moment when Nathan zipped past. Skalbrooke riders were thus holding the first four places.

It was also how the race ended. Greg remained completely unapproachable, in a competitive sense; what's more, his victory was so easy that Greg didn't even have to boast about his prowess! It was all too evident to everybody – and particularly the home side. But not much in the way of congratulations was offered to the triumphant quartet by Linkland parents or officials. Their attitude appeared to be one of resentment, not admiration.

Adrian was the only rider who voiced an opinion in the hearing of the Skalbrooke boys. 'Just a fluke, that's all,' he said indignantly. 'If I hadn't been knocked out of the race by that thug who finished fourth I'd've won easily as usual. Next race I'll prove it.'

The 'thug' in question, Nat Pike, just laughed. No insult was going to affect his pleasant nature. The only thing that bothered Nat was that he hadn't finished in a higher position. He'd managed to catch up with Lee, though not overtake him; Lee himself had just been pipped for second place by Darren,

306

who'd ridden a masterly race to frustrate his brother. Lee was thoroughly annoyed with himself. He felt at home on the circuit and yet he'd failed to make the most of it. His only consolation was that Daz, like Greg, was taking his success very calmly; there wasn't a single taunt directed at 'little brother'.

'This lot just don't prepare properly,' Greg airily told his friends when they were all back in the pits having their bikes attended to before the start of the next Inters' event. 'I mean, listen to that old Yamaha over there: needs its pistons replaced, I reckon. Pistons need renewing every third or fourth meeting. Right, Dad?'

Harry Shearsmith laughed. 'Right, son. Glad to see you're imbibing some real mechanical knowledge at last. I keep telling you: riding isn't everything. Knowing what goes on under the frame counts just as much.'

The rider of the maligned Yamaha, who couldn't help overhearing this exchange, looked questioningly at *his* mechanic, who was also his father. And father nodded resignedly, admitting defeat. He'd hoped the pistons would last another race.

In preparation for the next race Greg helped himself to a couple of doughnuts and a thick wedge of cheese. 'Good fuel, that!' he remarked. 'It'll keep me way out in front again.'

This time, though, he didn't have things all his own way. His flying start was matched by Lee's and

307

for the first lap they rode side by side, absolutely level as if driven by the same chain. For neutral observers the battle for outright leadership was a fine spectacle for neither rider was willing to concede an inch to his opponent. The rise to the summit of the loop was taken at an astonishing speed. Lee, however, had the inside berth for the right-hander and he made that advantage count double by deliberately forcing Greg wide towards the tyre barrier. Greg was quite prepared to bounce off the tyres – but he couldn't push through them. With a flicker of his back wheel, instantly corrected, Lee seized the lead – and surged remorselessly away down the slope. A sharp drop always brought out the best in his riding: and his nerve. For once Greg had been out-witted by an opponent just as brave as himself.

Daz had just missed the break and was in the middle of the pack. But a worse fate had overtaken Rupert Johnstone. He stalled his engine and by the time he got into motion the rest of the field seemed to have abandoned him.

Rupert, who was riding the second of the two bikes he owned, managed to catch up with the tail-enders by the middle of the second lap. By then, though, he knew he was in a hopeless position so far as winning the race was concerned, especially when it became clear that two of the Skalbrooke riders were setting a scorching pace again. This time, he decided in a burst of resentment, they weren't going to be allowed to get away with it. He personally would stop them.

Because, naturally enough, Adrian was in the group behind the trail-blazers, Rupert couldn't call on his support; so, instead, he looked for a crony among the stragglers. He soon found him in Jason Radford. Jason had no talent as a motocrosser and he was inclined to fool about, even in the middle of a race. Rupert succeeded in signalling his intentions as Lee, still closely attended by Greg, bore down on them. Rupert and Jason were about to be lapped.

Lee switched from side to side on the straights, seeking an opening. One of the problems with this track was its dangerous narrowness in many places, particularly on the spirals. That was why, of course, it favoured front-runners. Normally, hopeless tail-enders gave way when the race leader wanted to overtake. But this pair seemed determined to frustrate him. Riding side-by-side they kept coming together like pincers whenever Lee attempted to squeeze between them. He was getting angrier by the metre.

On an acute bend Lee dropped back deliberately, allowing them to draw ahead. Then he went down another gear, rapidly building up power for another thrust that this time must carry him past them. Then, just as he launched himself, the pair in front collided with each other through sheer carelessness and lack of control over their machines.

Luckily for him, Jason fell to the side of the track,

still attached to his bike. He was used to falling, sometimes as a deliberate comic act, and so he didn't hurt himself. Rupert was unlucky. He was thrown from his machine by the force of the impact and damaged an elbow. His Yamaha toppled over right in the centre of the track.

Lee was already too close to the Yamaha to avoid it. His line took him right over it and, oddly, it was the handlebars that took the brunt of the assault. They collapsed and were beyond repair. Lee's bike shook and wobbled but, somehow, he held it together. In a matter of seconds he was riding as if nothing had happened. Overcoming Rupert's horizontal Yamaha was little different, in race terms, from overcoming any other awkward obstacle in his path.

Greg was less fortunate. The scattering of bikes and bodies impeded him to such an extent that he skidded to a halt. Spectators were already converging on the scene, some even rushing across the track, before Greg was able to get going again and resume the race. A furious parent tried to force him to stop but Greg eluded the man. Far worse incidents than this were regular features of the racing at Skalbrooke. Greg couldn't see anything to fuss about. His only worry was that someone had managed to nip past him and thus Greg was now in third place. When he saw that it was Adrian Linthwaite he was really annoyed. It was bad enough being baulked by two of the Linkland lads. He didn't want to finish behind another.

Yet, hard as he tried, Greg was unable to catch up with Adrian: just as Adrian was unable to overhaul the flying Lee Parnaby. It was some consolation for the home side that at least one of their riders had taken second place. But it was no consolation to a group of parents who, incensed by the incident involving Rupert Johnstone, wanted the race to be declared void. They argued that such 'irresponsible and inconsiderate behaviour by a rider' – they meant Lee – should be punished severely.

Hastily the officials organised a committee meeting to be held immediately. Lee had his fingers crossed – and his team-mates' support. He was convinced he had done nothing wrong. The attitude of the parents had the tang of sour grapes: if Adrian had been the winner the matter would surely never have been raised.

After ten minutes of deep discussion the secretary announced that the result of the race would stand. No rules had been broken. The Skalbrooke contingent cheered. Greg was all for doing a victory dance in the pits until his father pointed out that wouldn't be seemly in the circumstances. Lee had a great deal to be pleased about: not only had he won the race, he'd got his revenge over Greg and beaten Daz out of sight. He intended to repeat the treatment on the second day of the Linkland Cove Motocross Club's Special Open Meeting.

Just as he was about to pass some comment to Greg

as they toasted each other in lemonade, Adrian Linthwaite and Rupert Johnstone sidled up to them.

'Don't laugh too loud,' Adrian warned them. 'We'll get our revenge tomorrow.'

'Or before,' Rupert muttered darkly.

Eight

For the second successive evening Lee, Greg and Darren dined out in style at the *Pizzeria* in Linkland Cove. This time, however, they didn't have the company of Mr Shearsmith: he'd gone off to spend a few hours with his friend Kel Gibson who owned, in addition to caravans, a holiday cottage a few miles along the coast from Linkland. 'My dad's mate is a property tycoon, you see,' Greg boasted, and there didn't seem to be any doubt about that. Harry Shearsmith, hinting that he might be returning quite late that evening, had provided ample money for their meal and entertainment in his absence.

As there was no one present to suggest they varied their diet, they chose, and speedily devoured, exactly the same dishes they'd tried the previous evening. Then they lingered over Cokes, debating how they should spend their free time. Darren favoured hiring a boat and 'doing a bit of fishing in the bay – it's great at night. We'll catch loads of fish and then we can sell it. Make a pile of money, like the tycoon your dad knows, Greg.' But Greg, who was in charge of the spending money and refused to share it out, dismissed that idea as boring. Lee would have been happy to see Daz go off on his own, to fish or to do anything else he wanted; but Greg over-ruled that suggestion, too. He believed his father had expected them to stay together.

'I quite fancy going roller-skating – must be plenty of that sort of action in a holiday place,' said Lee. Minutes earlier he had been intending to suggest a swim. Then Daz had mentioned the sea and that had put him off the idea.

'You just want to go somewhere to meet girls!' Darren remarked instantaneously. 'That's what you fancy, little brother.'

'Rubbish!' Lee shot back. But he could feel himself going red. Daz could always be relied on to say the wrong thing at the wrong time. Lee began to work out how they might manage to get rid of him that evening.

'Come on, let's get out of here,' said Greg hurriedly. He didn't want another war to break out between the brothers. Paying the bill with a flourish and then waving away the change with a grandiloquent gesture, he led the way out – and then had a brainwave. 'I know – we'll go to Fun-o-rama! Can't imagine why I didn't think of it before. You never know, Daz, you might just win a goldfish in a bowl. Lot easier than

315

dragging up some old cod from the bottom of the sea!'

Lee's spirits rose. He, too, had forgotten that Link-land Cove possessed its own fairground, located just off the promenade on the far side of the harbour. At this time of the year the place was likely to be packed out, so there was a good chance he and Greg could 'lose' Darren. His brother would surely be happier on his own, anyway.

Eager as ever to get something back for his outlay, even when it wasn't his own money he was spending, Daz wanted to have a go on all the games that offered a prize, whether cash or trash. Eventually, to cut off Daz's moans that this fun spot wasn't living up to its name as far as he was concerned, Greg doled out a few coins. For his own money, Greg wanted sheer thrills: rides in the whirling, hurling, stomach-swirling fly-ing machines that resembled oval capsules at the end of flexible steel sticks. Lee didn't accompany him. In his view, such sensations didn't compare with those of motocross.

After his second ride on that contraption Greg was, literally, in a giddy mood. He came down the steps from the exit in a jerky, sideways-on style, as though completely disorientated by his experience in the sky. Lee, who'd been watching from beside a nearby darts stall, laughed. It was impossible to tell whether Greg was play-acting or really suffering from a dislocated brain. Greg, having reached level ground, continued

316

to spin crazily, bumping into a strolling couple as he did so.

The couple didn't seem to mind, obviously regarding it as part of the fun of the fair. But Lee could see trouble looming up if Greg crashed into anyone less tolerant of his clowning, if that's what it was. So he moved smartly to grab Greg and steer him away from a collision course. Greg, still on a high, grabbed him round the waist and attempted to spin him round, as if they were dancing partners. This time they both bumped into somebody.

'Hey, cut it out!' the victim protested. Then came recognition: 'Oh, I might have guessed it was you two causing trouble again . . .'

Lee turned and discovered that they'd collided with Adrian Linthwaite. With him, and licking a huge cornet of ice-cream, was Rupert Johnstone.

Greg just laughed. 'You two should have learned to keep out of our way by now! You're bound to come off second-best when you meet us.'

Adrian scowled. His face was as thin as Rupert's was round and he had a trick of raising one eyebrow, the left, when he was about to speak. His hair stood up in a tuft like a salute at the front. Rather to Lee's surprise, Adrian was still wearing white shorts, though there wasn't much heat left in the day at that late hour. The moon had been out for some time, illuminating a remarkably clear sky.

'You think you can get away with anything, don't

you?' Adrian asked at last. His tone was hostile.

'Naturally, we're the best around here at anything,' Greg responded with another grin. 'I mean, we've *proved* it, haven't we?'

'Only by knocking people over and smashing their bikes – that's how,' Rupert said savagely. He looked directly at Lee, his eyes like slits.

Lee shrugged. 'Greg's just said it. You got in my way, deliberately I reckon. So I couldn't help riding over your bike.'

'You just didn't care *what* you did. You're a maniac!' Rupert continued.

318

Before Lee could defend himself Daz suddenly appeared on the scene. He really had been trying, but without success, to win a goldfish by tossing a table tennis ball into a narrow-necked jar. What he failed to judge now was the mood of the encounter taking place just in front of him. With an unusual burst of exuberance he jumped forward, trying to put his arm round Adrian's shoulders in a mock wrestling hold.

Adrian's legs were thin but strong. He staggered but didn't fall. Daz, off-balance, tumbled awkwardly against Rupert, causing him to drop his ice-cream. Rupert, already full of anger because of all the set-

319

backs of the day, swung a fierce punch at Daz. It landed on the shoulder but, somehow, Darren just managed to keep his feet. He wasn't hurt but he was surprised: very surprised. Yet Rupert hadn't finished his attack.

He was on the point of delivering a second punch when Lee pounced. With one cutting blow of his hand he knocked aside Rupert's arm. Then, as Rupert tried to retaliate, Lee dropped to one knee, grabbed his opponent's leg by ankle and knee, twisted and tugged – and brought Rupert crashing to the ground.

Retaining a hold on his leg so that he couldn't get away, Lee held a fist poised above Rupert's throat. 'You touch him again and you'll get this,' he warned. 'Understand?'

Rupert nodded his understanding and acceptance of defeat; and then Lee released him.

The speed and the outcome of Lee's reaction stunned them all for a few moments. Daz looked at his younger brother in a kind of admiration that almost amounted to awe. At that moment it didn't occur to him that he hadn't really needed anyone to defend him. Greg, too, was impressed. He'd always known that Lee was tough and resilient; but the way in which he'd dealt with Rupert, a boy much heavier than himself, was a revelation.

Adrian was the only one who appeared unaffected by the incident. It hadn't occurred to him to retaliate

320

when Daz jumped on him. Brawling wasn't Adrian's style. While Rupert was suffering at the hands of Lee his friend and team-mate had been thinking constructively.

'You lot from Skalbrooke think you can beat us at anything, don't you?' Adrian told them coldly. He didn't wait for any reply. 'You beat us on the track this afternoon because you had a lot of luck. But you'll need more than luck to beat Rupert and me on the harbour-and-promenade circuit. You'll need more nerve than any of you three possess to ride that at night. I bet you daren't have a go at that.'

Greg was predictably puzzled. 'Harbour-and-promenade circuit? What's that then?'

Adrian exchanged glances with Rupert, now rapidly recovering his composure and eager to demonstrate that he didn't lose at everything. The thought of gaining his revenge over Lee Parnaby swamped any doubts he had about Adrian's plans. He would go along with whatever Adrian suggested.

'It's our own private motocross route, the toughest in Britain,' Adrian said. 'But it can only be ridden at night – the middle of the night. You need plenty of moonlight and we've got that. So, are you three going to take us on tonight?'

Lee was the one who didn't hesitate. By now he was in a state of euphoria.

'Of course we will! So come on, tell us all the details.'

Nine

As they wheeled their motocross bikes through the caravan park Lee was praying that they wouldn't meet Harry Shearsmith returning from his evening out. Greg had insisted that his father would thoroughly approve of their competing in a midnight motocross. Lee thought otherwise. No adult would permit boys of their age to do what they were planning to do in the next half-hour.

So far luck had been completely on their side. A key to the transporter had been left in the caravan for emergencies and so there was no problem about getting at the bikes and their riding-gear. It was already late by the time they returned to the caravan and there weren't many people about; those that were still up hadn't the energy or interest to ask any questions. Even so, the three of them agreed it would be inviting trouble to start up the machines before they were clear of the park.

None of them had thought of ducking the chal-

322

lenge so unexpectedly thrown down by Adrian (or, if so, hadn't dared mention it, sensing the scorn it would provoke). The excitements of the day and evening hadn't tired them at all. In the caravan, strapping on their protectors and leathers and boots, they'd exclaimed how fresh they felt, how eager they were to tackle this mysterious moonlit obstacle course. They boasted about the finishing-order. Each one of them believed the winner would be himself.

The roar of the engine had never sounded so loud to Lee's ears as it did when at last he started it up. Nervously he glanced round to see whether anyone was watching: but the shadows in the hollows of the headland betrayed no one's presence. They were to meet Adrian and Rupert at Westvale, a point on the cliff close to the start of the official motocross circuit. Lee couldn't help wondering whether the Linkland riders would really turn up. It was quite possible that the plan for the midnight race was a hoax devised on the spur on the moment by Adrian Linthwaite. Perhaps Adrian and Rupert were lying in their beds, laughing uncontrollably at the thought of the three of them turning out for absolutely nothing.

Daz, who had eyes like an owl's, was the first to spot them as they coasted round the rim of the dip in the ground that was signposted Westvale. There was a note of relief in his voice as he pointed them out. It hadn't occurred to Lee that his brother had shared his worries. So far Daz had been fairly quiet about the whole venture. For once he wasn't the elder and leader; he was the outsider of a threesome. For that reason alone, he was determined to be the victor of the race that was about to be run. He'd suffered two defeats already that day. A third would be disastrous.

Adrian was sitting astride his bike, waiting for them; Rupert was checking the rear tyre of his machine, the third choice of the three he'd ridden that day. Neither of them hinted that they hadn't expected the Skalbrooke trio to turn up. Instead, Adrian immediately launched into a description of the route they'd take: it was, he declared, perfectly straightforward. The race would consist of one lap only, down to the harbour and back to the starting point.

'We go down this broad path to the edge of the cliff,' he explained tersely. 'The path then becomes a zigzag walkway, used by a lot of courting couples. Shouldn't be many of them about now. That takes us right on to the beach – level stretch of sand. Then up on to the Promenade by the slipway for little boats. There's another straight stretch on to the harbour wall and we go down that. Do a U-turn at the end by the lifebelts. Then head back the way we've come. First home is the champion!'

Everyone allowed that to sink in before a question was asked. Then Greg inquired what would happen if they met anyone.

'Avoid 'em! Just don't stop for anything or anyone.

You'll be faster than them so there should be no problems. People who see us won't know who we are.'

It was then that Lee realised what was different about the bikes Adrian and Rupert were riding: the club numbers had been removed. But there wasn't time for the Skalbrooke motocrossers to do likewise. Adrian was telling them that it was time to line up. He would raise his hand: and as soon as it dropped the race started. In order to be seen he edged fractionally ahead of his rivals. Helmets were adjusted, engines revved. Tension crept into every active muscle. No

one thought about danger: for danger was part of every motocross event. Danger always rode with them.

Adrian's arm chopped down!

They surged away as one and it was several metres before the line really broke up. Remarkably, no one had attempted to anticipate the signal: and Adrian hadn't taken advantage of his role as official starter.

Rupert was the first to show in front. Normally his initial acceleration wasn't of the best but this time he'd got it exactly right. As he moved into the middle of the track he was just over a bike-length ahead of Lee and Adrian. To his consternation, Greg was soon in fifth place. Then he decided it wasn't the worst place to be; after all, now he could see where everyone else was heading on this unexplored circuit.

His white helmet acting like a guiding light, Rupert was first into the zigzagged walkway, narrow but firm of surface, the double seats for weary walkers fortunately recessed in order not to take up vital standing-space. There was no opportunity for anyone to overtake on that descent: the only hope of improving one's position would come if someone crashed. No one did. Instinctively, every rider allowed for survival. The race would come on the beach and on the Promenade, in both directions.

Without being aware of it, they passed a boy and his girl, embracing on a seat, and then swopped the hard-packed earth of the path for the freedom of the

sands. The leader went out to the right, as if in search
of a firmer surface, one recently washed by the waves.
Lee, instantaneously moving up a gear, went after
him, apparently heading for the glistening sea. He
was confident he could take Rupert whenever he
wanted to with all this space at his command. Faintly,
he was aware that Adrian was taking a parallel course,
but on the landward side of Rupert. The remaining
two riders decided to sit on Rupert's tail.

Suddenly, Rupert's bike faltered. Almost immediately afterwards, there was a change in the engine-
note. Lee, edging out to the right, was already splash-
ing through water when Rupert slid sideways as the
front wheel sank in treacherous sand. In the same
moment Lee felt a dip under his own wheels and,
simultaneously, the machine lost power.

Hastily, he went down the gears but it felt now as
though he were trying to steer through a vat of por-
ridge. He needed extra strength just to keep going.
Anxiously, he switched direction, turning towards
the shore to find firmer going. Out of the corner of his
eye he saw Rupert getting to his knees, struggling to
drag his bike from the gluepot he'd entered; and, way
over to the left, Adrian was speeding serenely ahead.
Aware of the dangers on that stretch of sand, he'd
taken a completely different course.

Somehow – and afterwards he still wasn't sure how –
Lee kept going. All his hard work in weight-training
and muscle-building was paying off as, physically, he

327

lifted his bike through the worst of the soggy stretches. Behind him, Greg, too, was in trouble; unlike Lee, he hadn't sensed it soon enough and so thought that sheer speed would carry him through the worst of the conditions. It didn't. Soon a mini-quicksand claimed him. So the field for the midnight motocross was reduced to three.

Adrian was taking a curved course to avoid a groyne, a broken line of timber designed to retain washed-up sand and save it from the sea. Lee realised that his best hope of cutting back Adrian's lead was to find a gap in that battered wooden fence. To his rear, Daz was thinking the same: and wondering when he should attempt to overtake his brother.

In places the sand, flung against the groyne, had piled up like a ramp. It was at such a point that Lee aimed himself in his determination not to allow Adrian to extend his lead. Bike and rider were flowing again like a tide as Lee punched through the wall from the incline and went into the void on the other side. The drop was steeper than he'd imagined but his technique for coping with downhill jumps stood up to this testing examination. Surging away from the landing-point, he saw that he had sliced fifty metres from Adrian's advantage. He wasn't aware that the two of them were the only ones effectively left in the race.

Daz had followed precisely in his brother's wheel-track to clear the groyne. What he hadn't bargained for was the depth of the drop on the other side. Riding at a fractionally slower pace than Lee, he came down at a steeper angle and the impact flung him from the saddle. Because he landed on sand, he wasn't hurt. But by the time he was properly re-united with his machine he was out of touch with the race. After brushing damp sand from his goggles, he dejectedly set off to follow the pair ahead of him. At least he wanted to say he'd completed the course. Then a bright thought struck him: maybe Lee and Adrian would crash before getting back to Westvale; if they did, then Daz still had a chance of winning the race. Cheerfully, he moved up a gear.

Adrian, who'd been congratulating himself on his smart thinking in taking the inside track, was astonished to see how close his pursuer was. Because he'd been concentrating on his own route he'd not seen Lee blast his way over the groyne and so make up a great deal of ground. Now, as they neared the incline leading to the Promenade, Adrian knew he'd have to ride like someone possessed to keep his rival at bay.

With his quarry squarely in his sights, Lee settled down to a fast and steady ride. The leap through the sand barrier had convinced him that this was his night. After those anxious moments in what he'd thought was quicksand he knew he could survive anything. For the moment he was content to sit on Adrian's tail, putting pressure on his rival by keeping

329

so close but not trying to overtake. There was really no need to pull in front yet: he could do that whenever he felt like it.

Up on to the smooth, metalled Promenade they roared and seconds later Lee was jolted out of his complacency for, without warning, Adrian swerved violently to the left: and then back again. He'd acted to avoid a pedestrian, a man enjoying a nocturnal stroll with his dog. It was the mongrel that worried Lee. Jumping up and snapping fiercely, it seemed determined to seize Lee's leg and pull him off his bike.

Lee's inclination was to kick out at the dog: but he remembered just in time that he was the one in the wrong, by riding across a pedestrian area. If he injured the dog he'd be in very serious trouble should its owner succeed in identifying him. So, zigzagging like an Olympic skier, he managed to evade the hound. But that manoeuvre cost him a few lengths in his pursuit of Adrian, now heading for the harbour-wall. Lee prayed that they wouldn't meet any more people on that narrow walkway round the harbour, crowded with yachts and fishing smacks and pleasure-craft. Most of the late-night revellers had gone home and only a few lights were showing in the cottages and boarding-houses on the far side of the bay.

The racers sped across the grid of shadows formed by the boats' masts and then, by the row of lifebelts

330

under a parapet, they turned through 180 degrees: and it was then they both knew they were the only ones left in the race. Even Daz had still not reached the harbour-wall.

As they left the boats in their wake and regained the Promenade Lee looked about anxiously. He didn't want another encounter with the man and his mongrel. But, to his relief, they'd gone, sensibly seeking shelter behind an ice-cream kiosk. From there, though, the man fired a volley of insults at the 'crazy, speed-mad young hooligans'.

Back on the beach the duellists rode high above the tide-line. Deliberately Lee stayed a bike-length behind Adrian, sure that he had the power to surge ahead whenever he decided to use it. Then, without being aware that they were coming up, both riders found themselves on a sharp series of stutter bumps, hard-packed sand formed into ridges like ribs by a procession of tiny streams. Lee raised himself from the saddle instantly, riding with impeccable balance by keeping his weight in the middle of the machine. These were conditions he'd encountered on many tracks and so he treated them with composure.

Not so Adrian, for they were new to him. His machine began to buck like a furious horse and Adrian had no idea how to cope with the jolts and slides. The outcome was inevitable. Thrown high by a particularly severe bounce, the bike came down almost sideways on to the ridge. Desperately Adrian tried to wrench it round by strength alone. But the drive from the rear-wheel simply caught him completely off-balance and Adrian was catapulted across the sand in one direction as the bike went off in the other.

Until he reached the last of the stutter bumps Lee had his knees pressed against the tank, keeping a low profile to beat the drag and absorbing the severity of the juddering of the fork through his arms. After that, he could afford to cruise all the way to the finishing-point. He was in such an exultant mood that he felt like shouting for joy. So he shouted, several

times! By now, there was only the sea and the sand to hear him. *'Key-AI!'*

Not once on that most testing stretch of bumps had he felt so much as a twinge of protest from his muscles. Probably he'd never been fitter in his life. It was a glorious feeling. There was no prize awaiting him when he reached Westvale and so completed the circuit of the Linkland Cove midnight motocross. But there was the glory of being the winner, the easiest possible winner. Daz was somewhere in the distance and in the dark. He wasn't the tiger of this or any other track. Lee was.

By now, Adrian, injured only in pride and not in body, was back on his bike. He would finish second. The others would follow eventually.

Lee killed his engine and lifted off his goggles and helmet. Then he sat, waiting patiently for all his rivals to catch him up.